Kate Coombs

THE RUNAWAY DRAGON

When Meg's dragon, Laddy, flies away from home, she knows she must go on a quest to find him. But she hasn't counted on her parents, the king and queen of Greeve, sending ten guardsmen along. Fortunately, she is also accompanied by her best friends: Dilly, a lady-in-waiting and a cool head in any crisis not involving heights; Cam, a gardener's assistant who knows the exact value of a brick shed filled with sausages; Nort, a skinny guardsman who has never given much thought to crows; and Lex, a young wizard with bad taste in horses, magic carpets, and sorceresses. Of course, Meg's quest goes topsy-turvy once she enters the enchanted forest—and her adventure is just beginning. What's more, meeting up with the dashing bandit Bain again isn't at all what she expected. Will this princess be able to rescue herself, let alone anybody else?

In *The Runaway Princess*, Meg and her friends defeated a pack of princes. Now they're going to need swordplay, magic, and a whole lot of courage to find Laddy and get back home!

KATE COOMBS is the author of *The Runaway Princess*, an ALA Notable Book. She lives in Los Angeles, California.

THE RUNAWAY
DRAGON

The
RUNAWAY
DRAGON

Kate Coombs

FARRAR, STRAUS AND GIROUX
NEW YORK

Copyright © 2009 by Kathryn Coombs
Distributed in Canada by Douglas & McIntyre Ltd.
Printed in the United States of America
Designed by Jaclyn Sinquett
First edition, 2009
1   3   5   7   9   10   8   6   4   2

www.fsgkidsbooks.com

Library of Congress Cataloging-in-Publication Data
Coombs, Kate.
     The runaway dragon / Kate Coombs.— 1st ed.
          p.   cm.
     Sequel to: The runaway princess.
     Summary: When her beloved dragon Laddy runs away from the
castle, Princess Meg and some of her friends embark on a quest to
find him and bring him home.
     ISBN-13: 978-0-374-36361-1
     [1. Fairy tales.   2. Princesses—Fiction.   3. Dragons—Fiction.]
I. Title.

PZ8.C788 Ru 2010
[Fic]—dc22

                                        2008034362

For my sister, Loni, who used to say,
"Tell me a story!"

THE RUNAWAY
DRAGON

PROLOGUE

AT FIRST MEG VISITED LADDY A LOT, RIDING HER horse from the castle through the Witch's Wood to Hookhorn Farm, where her friend Cam's sister lived. Meg would sit by the fire in the big farm-house kitchen and talk with Janna, scratching Laddy behind his ears and then along his little scarlet-and-amber dragon back. Not that Laddy was so little any-more. He was growing quickly, feasting on sausages and stew chickens at Hookhorn Farm. If Meg's father, King Stromgard, hadn't made provision for Laddy's keep, the baby dragon would have eaten Janna out of house and home.

When Meg had found Laddy in his mother's cave, surrounded by dragon treasure, she had discovered that she could talk to him in her mind. He had never answered with words, but she could tell by the way he responded that the little dragon understood her—a handy thing, since Meg and Cam were trying very hard to save Laddy from a pack of princes.

Of course, the princes were long gone. A year had passed, and Laddy wasn't a baby anymore. He proved it one bright morning while Meg was visiting the farmhouse. *Such a beautiful boy!* she thought at him.

Yes, I am, she heard in her mind.

"Did you *talk*?" Meg said out loud, startled. Laddy merely blinked at her with his black eyes slit with gold.

"What?" called Janna, bustling around the kitchen.

"Nothing. Just talking to Laddy." Meg tried again, this time in her head. *Laddy, did you talk?*

Nothing. But Meg knew of a surefire conversational gambit for young dragons. *Laddy, are you hungry?*

There was a brief silence. Then she heard, *Hungry for gold.* Meg grinned and reached for the pouch at her side.

Janna had stopped her bustling to look at the two. "What is it?"

"I think he wants a gold coin to play with," Meg told her.

"I'd like a few coins to play with myself," Janna said.

Meg opened the leather pouch and took out a gold coin. It had her father's profile on it, looking much more handsome than in real life. Whoever had a nose that aquiline?

The young dragon stretched his head forward, watching Meg's hand as she brought the coin closer to him. *Mine,* he told her in her mind.

Yours, Meg agreed.

Laddy opened his small oven of a mouth and took the coin delicately from Meg's palm with his slender scarlet tongue.

Are you really going to eat it? Meg asked.

That's when Meg first heard a dragon's giggle. *No,* Laddy thought at her. *Silly princess.* Laddy reached out one of his clawed front feet and placed it on Meg's knee, retracting the claws so they wouldn't hurt her. *Mine,* he said again.

Yes, Laddy, Meg thought, *I'm your*—she hesitated to say "owner"—*friend.* Meg's father called Laddy her pet, but Meg knew nobody really owned a dragon. For that matter, nobody she knew had even *tried* to own one.

Laddy is a baby name, the little dragon told her.

Meg looked at him more carefully. She used to be able to drape Laddy across her lap, or at least her feet, and now he was as long as she was tall, not counting his crenellated tail. His butter-colored wings often crashed into the furniture, and last week, according to Janna, they had swept three hours' worth of dinner preparations onto the floor. Janna had warned Meg that soon Laddy would have to stay in the barn all day. He was simply getting too big for the house.

Meg wished, not for the first time, that she could take Laddy back to the castle, but her parents wouldn't hear of it.

New name? Laddy prodded. *Grand grownup name?*

Meg *had* promised to give him a better name some-day, since "Laddy" wasn't exactly her idea. But she'd got-ten used to it by now. They all had. *You're not grownup yet,* Meg told him.

Laddy huffed out a little cloud of smoke, clearly dis-satisfied.

All right. I'll think of one soon, Meg said.

At that Laddy smiled dragonishly and settled down for yet another nap, the gold coin shining between his two front feet.

The next time Meg saw Laddy, he was sulking over being banished to the barn. He wouldn't look at her, wouldn't even talk to her. Then Meg got really busy with her les-sons, especially magic, her worst subject. Meg didn't go out to Hookhorn Farm for a long while.

That was probably a mistake.

I

MEG PUT THE BACK OF ONE HAND TO HER FORE-
head and leaned against the windowsill of her
chamber, looking out over the royal vegetable
garden to the city of Crown, her imagination flying
across the rest of the Kingdom of Greeve and into the
wide world beyond. Her green gown flowed gracefully
down her semi-slim sides. Her golden tresses—well, her
light brown tresses—flowed almost as gracefully down her
back. "Alas and alack," Meg said in a breathless voice,
"will no one come to take me away from this foul place?"
She snickered. *Boring* place was more like it.

Meg's mother was worried about the lack of princes
coming to court her daughter. Meg wasn't. She was more
interested in coming up with a way of convincing her
parents to let her go on a quest.

Meg left the window to change into a more service-
able skirt, tunic, and short, soft boots. She clipped her

hair back and buckled on her sword, then headed downstairs for her first class of the day. She nearly crashed into Dilly, who was coming up the stairs. Dilly used to be Meg's maid, but now she was Meg's one and only lady-in-waiting. "Sword lessons?" Dilly asked, after neatly stepping out of Meg's way.

"Sword lessons," Meg answered. Swordplay was Meg's favorite class, followed by statesmanship, a class taught by the austere Lady Fralen. Meg had expected to hate it, but to her amazement, she was pretty good at diplomacy and sort of liked it. Years of trying to get around her mother so she could hunt for frogs or roam the woods with Cam the gardener's boy had taught her a lot about smooth talking, and it turned out that was what statesmanship was. That and figuring out what the other person wanted.

Meg tried not to think about her other classes for today, etiquette and magic and dance. She was bad at all three.

"Lucky you," said Dilly.

"Why, where are you going?"

Dilly made a face. "Eugenia invited me again." Queen Istilda's ladies-in-waiting were trying to turn Dilly into a fluffbrain, but so far Dilly was resisting.

"You can tell me about it tonight."

"Oh, I will!" Dilly gave a positively evil little laugh. Her reenactments of the embroidery-and-gossip sessions put on by the queen's ladies were getting better with practice, though Meg suspected Dilly left out some of the talk about Meg not being courted by anyone. Laughing more normally, Dilly went on up the stairs, her brown gown and tidy black hair looking suitably demure.

Meg's swordplay instructor, Master Zolis, was already warming up when she arrived. Meg greeted him and began going through the stretches herself in a shaft of sunlight from one of the unadorned windows along the outer wall.

Master Zolis wasn't a big man. In fact, he looked nearly as unassuming as Garald, the king's dull prime minister. Master Zolis's hair had disappeared entirely on the top of his head, and his shoulders weren't particularly broad. But everyone in the castle knew that the swordmaster wielded his weapon as if it were a wizard's wand. All of the guardsmen stood in line for the chance to practice with him. Meg got her very own lessons twice a week.

Meg smiled a little as she leaned over her left leg and touched the worn wooden floor. As a teacher, Master Zolis wasn't one to dish out praise just because his pupil was a princess, but after Meg's last lesson, he had said, "Not bad." Meg had been treasuring the words ever since. Practicing in her room had paid off. She'd only cut her bed hangings once, over on the back of the bed where it didn't show from the door.

Master Zolis was usually a man of more sword strokes than words, but today he had something to say. He gestured to Meg to sit on a bench beside him. "Princess Margaret, you have learned enough to put on a very pretty exhibition match."

Meg hoped this was a compliment, but before she could say thank you, the swordmaster went on. "However, what will you do if someone really wants to kill you?"

"Isn't that what you've been teaching me for?"

Master Zolis shook his head, causing his bald spot to catch the light. "What I've given you is a mere beginning. If someone does try to kill you, you're best off running away."

Meg thought of all the imaginary monsters and dark sorcerers she'd been killing in her room lately and frowned. "That's not very heroic."

"No, it isn't. Now think, Princess. If an archer shoots an arrow at you, what do you do?"

"Duck," Meg said, not sure where Master Zolis was going with this.

"Very good." Master Zolis got up again and began pacing back and forth, swinging his sword as if it were much lighter than it looked, as light as Meg's sword. "And if a wizard throws a spell at you?"

"Duck?"

"Certainly. What if a very large man with twenty years of experience at sword swinging comes after you?"

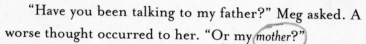

Meg sighed. "I should run away."

"That is correct."

"Have you been talking to my father?" Meg asked. A worse thought occurred to her. "Or my mother?"

"Not at all. But instructors are famous for dosing their students with wisdom or, in this case, plain common sense." He grinned. "I've seen how fierce you get in practice."

Wasn't that a good thing? "But if there's always someone better than me around the corner . . ."

"Or simply more eager to strike a deathblow than you are," Master Zolis suggested.

"Or that. Then why bother studying?" Meg stuck out her lower jaw a bit.

Master Zolis's eyes twinkled. He gave his sword an intricate flourish. "As I've often told you, swordsmanship is an art. Come, Princess. Let me see the Seventeenth Griffin."

Meg got up and unsheathed her own sword, which was looking far more ordinary at the moment, as if it had been listening to the swordmaster's speech. Meg adjusted her grip on the silver sword hilt, relishing the cool feel of it in her hand. She set her left foot at a slight angle to her right and then lunged forward, twirling to her left at the last second and then dropping to one knee so that the tip of her sword rested just below her instructor's chin. Or that was the plan, anyway. Instead she felt a slight rush of air as the swordmaster moved, not acting at all like the opponent of Meg's imagination. Meg ended up flat on her back with Master Zolis's foot lightly resting on her inner elbow and her sword halfway across the room.

"Much better," the swordmaster said, moving his foot aside. "Hop up and do it again."

If magic had been any easier for her, Meg's least favorite class would have been royal etiquette, in which Mistress Mintz instructed Meg far too thoroughly in court protocol. All Meg could do was smile grimly and say, "Yes, Mistress Mintz," or "No, Mistress Mintz," as she tried to remember the prissy details that accompanied her royal status like so many chaperones. Just because she'd run away from home and acted in various unseemly ways a year ago didn't mean she was completely lacking in courtly graces. But her mother had thought so, and that was the reason for Mistress Mintz.

Meg approached the parlor where Mistress Mintz reigned over a little kingdom of lace doilies and flowered armchairs. Meg preferred real flowers herself—they were sloppy and friendly and swayed in the wind. Of course, nothing dared to move out of its place in Mistress Mintz's parlor. The complete opposite of the swordmaster's austere domain, it was stuffed with ruffles and furbelows and amazingly adorable large-eyed knick-knacks. Meg shortened her steps automatically as she came through the door.

It seemed to her that the etiquette teacher should dress in pale-colored flowers to match the decor, but as usual Mistress Mintz was wearing a tense black dress. She greeted Meg with chilly formality, asked her in appalled tones to take off her sword, and informed her that the topic of today's lesson was curtsies. "Now, Princess Margaret, let me see you curtsy," the etiquette instructor said. Her small eyes narrowed, anticipating Meg's least mistake.

Still, Meg dipped with such care that she really thought she'd gotten it right.

Mistress Mintz pursed her lips. "And to whom was that curtsy directed?"

"Um—to you?"

"To you, Mistress Mintz," the woman prompted.

"To you, Mistress Mintz," Meg repeated.

"No!" Mistress Mintz snapped. "I should certainly hope not!"

"Why ever not?" Meg asked.

"Why ev—" Mistress Mintz began.

"Why ever not, Mistress Mintz?" Meg said, trying again.

"I can't imagine you are entirely unaware that there are eleven types of curtsies," Meg's instructor announced. "Did you not read the lesson pages?"

"Oh, it's just that . . . what happened is . . . I was busy with other assignments," Meg said, twiddling her skirt nervously.

"Princesses do not make excuses," Mistress Mintz said. Then she looked at Meg's hands pointedly. "And they do *not* fidget."

Meg wasn't about to tell her etiquette instructor that last night she was practicing the Seventeenth Griffin. Who had time for curtsies? You just bobbed, was all. As for the book, it was called *Royal Etiquette for Every Occasion,* and Meg couldn't think of a single occasion when she'd wanted to read it. She and Dilly had laughed about it on and off for weeks, and not just because all of the women in the book were dressed as if they'd lived a hundred years ago, with very high collars and low-hanging, round headdresses that made them resemble a bunch of turtles.

For now, all Meg said was, "I'm sorry, Mistress Mintz." She made an effort to talk the way she was supposed to. "Perhaps you would be so kind as to demonstrate the curtsies for me?"

Mistress Mintz gave Meg a tiny smile. "Very well."

To no one's surprise, it soon became clear that Meg couldn't tell the eleven curtsies apart. And she couldn't remember more than three or four of their names. This was probably because, instead of having wonderful names like the Seventeenth Griffin or Death Comes Swiftly, they were all named after noblewomen who had lived about a hundred years ago and looked like turtles.

"No, *this* is the Lady Evaline," Mistress Mintz said, curtsying deeply.

"I thought that was the Queen Violet."

Mistress Mintz's blue-gray hair quivered indignantly. "Hardly, my dear." When she said "my dear," it didn't sound endearing at all. "Watch closely."

Meg tried and tried. With a great deal of swooshing and swishing and only a little bobbing, Meg produced a fairly good imitation of the first two curtsies.

"That was adequate," the woman said.

Meg couldn't help letting out a dismal sigh.

"When a young lady avoids her responsibilities as a princess," Mistress Mintz said, looking down her nose at Meg, "she naturally finds herself lacking in the most basic of royal requirements."

"What do you mean?" Meg didn't like the sound of that.

"I mean that anyone who shirks her duty by leaving her assigned place and interfering with her father's princely competition may find that she is thereafter shunned by young men of quality."

Mistress Mintz had never before dared insult Meg this openly about her adventures. "Quality? Those princes would still be frogs if it weren't for me!" Meg said hotly. "How would you like to be locked in a tower and have your father offer half the kingdom and your hand in marriage to some buffoon in a crown?"

To Meg's astonishment, the etiquette teacher looked positively wistful at the thought. But the woman quickly recovered her famous dignity. "The idea of a princess rescuing the very creatures intended to be defeated by such a contest is simply shocking, as you well know."

"Gorba is a nice witch, and Laddy is a sweet little dragon!"

"Next I suppose you're going to defend those bandits," Mistress Mintz said in acid tones.

"They're gone now. They weren't that bad." Even if they *had* taken eleven chests filled with dragon treasure when they went.

The etiquette teacher shook her head sorrowfully. "Princess Margaret, the work ahead of us is *extensive*."

Frankly, Meg thought her teacher's remarks were far from polite. But there was no point in arguing. Meg kept quiet, hoping this would soon be over. Whereupon Mistress Mintz gave her a long speech about why manners were of the utmost importance, after which she assigned Meg to really, truly read the chapter on curtsies. And finally, they were finished. Which would have been very good news, if it didn't mean that it was time for Meg's magic lesson.

2

An hour later, while Meg was busy studying magic with Master Torskelly in his cluttered workroom, a dragon buzzed the castle. As Dilly was to tell Meg that afternoon, Nort had been staring at Dilly in the east hallway when the uproar started. Nort had been doing that a lot lately, and it was annoying Dilly no end. She was practically missing the days when the skinny apprentice guardsman used to alternately ignore her or tattle on her to her uncle, Guard Captain Hanak. Dilly was about to march up to Nort and tell him to stop it when a strange rushing noise was heard outside the window, followed quickly by an inhuman roar, a very human scream, a whoosh, and a smell of smoke.

Half the people in the hall ran to the windows; the other half ran away. Nort and Dilly met in the middle, where he tackled her manfully and threw her to the floor.

"Get off!" she yelled.

"I'm protecting you," he announced.

"Well, stop it!" Dilly spat, managing to say just what she'd been wanting to say about Nort's staring at her only a moment before. Dilly pulled free of her rescuer and hurried to the window, where she was treated to the sight of a red-and-gold tail flopping up over the battlements. "Dragon!" someone shouted rather obviously, and a volley of arrows sprayed the sky.

The tail looked familiar, Dilly thought. "Laddy?" she said.

"Meg's dragon?" Nort rushed to stand beside her.

The dragon seemed to fall backward. Everyone at the windows gasped, some hopefully and, in Dilly's case at least, others worriedly. Then the dragon spun itself about in midair and, thrusting against the castle wall with a back claw, launched off into furious flight.

The dragon wasn't huge, but it was a beauty, its underbelly and wings golden and its back scarlet touched with amber. It soared out of reach of the arrows, higher and higher, till it looked like a lost sunbeam and then disappeared altogether. "That *was* Laddy," Dilly whispered. Forgetting her annoyance, she turned to run. "We've got to find Meg!"

Meg's first thought was that she had conjured up something horrible. A few minutes earlier, she had been concentrating on her magic lesson, thinking maybe this time she would get her spell to work. Her magic tutor, for his part, had been thinking in a depressed, philosophical sort of way that some people who wanted to paint were color-blind, some people who wanted to sing were tone-deaf, and some people who wanted to make magic were— well, Princess Margaret. He did not say so, however, though the expression on his face was particularly eloquent.

"Not even close?" Meg asked woefully.

Master Torskelly shook his head. "No, Princess. Not a bit."

Meg peered down at the circle of spellwork. It *looked* just like the picture in the book. The hensleaf and the tickwort were in the right spots, as were a cricket and a bit of tapestry. Meg was also pretty sure she had said the spell properly: "Poppilin callifus haig." The spell just didn't do what it was supposed to: transform the cricket into a buttercup.

There was no help for it. Meg was abysmally bad at magic. Now, anyone can be incapable of magic, and that is what it means to be bad at magic. To be abysmally bad at magic, a person has to be able to cast a spell, but make it come out wrong every time.

For that reason, Meg's tutor waited anxiously, hoping the princess's spell wouldn't work at all. It was hard to tell. One of Meg's spells had seemed to fail, but a pitcher of cream in the next room was later found to have turned to seawater. And the twelfth third-floor housemaid had been more than a little distressed when another of Meg's attempts at magic had changed the woman's speech to the bloodthirsty cry of a gorebeast. They'd had to call in the boy wizard, Lex, to take care of that one.

Thbbbbbhbt! Meg heard, surely not in her head. "Sir?" Had her tutor really just given her the raspberry?! And behind her back?

"Yes?" Master Torskelly said, his voice as mild and cultured as ever.

"Did you speak or," Meg hesitated, "make a sound, just now?"

"Not at all. I know you need quiet to concentrate."

Maybe the poor old man was gassy. Or maybe she'd just imagined the sound. Meg began to rearrange her spell. Then a tumult filled the halls and poured in at the window.

"Now what?" Meg said.

Master Torskelly sighed for the fifth time that morning. "Come along. We'll find out what happened."

In the halls, everyone was rushing about and calling out the word "dragon."

Meg looked sideways at her tutor. "I don't think I could have conjured up a dragon."

They were just heading around the corner toward the throne room when Dilly caught up with them. "Meg! Laddy's gone!"

"Not before scaring everyone half to death," Nort added, skidding to a halt beside Dilly.

"Ha!" Meg said to her tutor. "I knew I hadn't conjured up a dragon!" Then she frowned. "What do you mean, Laddy? Not *Laddy*."

Dilly nodded. "He made someone scream and—I'm not sure what he did, except that they started shooting arrows at him and he flew away."

"Arrows!" Meg cried. "Was he hit?"

"I don't think so," Dilly told her.

They were nearly to the throne room now. Even from the hallway, Meg could hear voices grumbling and griping. Suddenly the king's voice roared out, worse than a dragon's: "Margaret!"

"Oops," Meg said. And she went to face her father.

When Meg walked in, King Stromgard was leaning forward in his ornate throne, looking tragically at a ragged something or other held up before him by two solemn guardsmen. As she got closer, Meg could smell a nasty charred scent. "Excuse me, but what is that thing, Father?"

The king finally met her eyes. "That is, or that was . . ." He cleared his throat and fell silent.

Queen Istilda spoke from her seat beside him. "It's what's left of the flag of Greeve."

"The *royal* flag that represented our proud kingdom," Meg's father elaborated.

"Oh," Meg said. "The flag Great-great-grandmother Ameliana embroidered? With the daisies and the, um, the dragon, and those little bent thingies?"

"Chevrons," said the queen.

The courtiers rumbled and hissed against the throne room's backdrop of heroic tapestries. Meg tried not to look at any of them. "What happened?" she asked, raising the inevitable.

"Your dragon happened," King Stromgard told her. "At least, *a* dragon happened, and I've just been informed it was your pet! The creature you *promised* would stay at that farm! Instead it flew over *my* castle—" The king turned to his captain of the guards. "What did it do, exactly?"

Looking more stern than usual, Hanak picked up the tale. "The dragon surprised Lady Lilac out picnicking on the green. Then it headed straight for the top of the north tower and burned the flag. Upon being targeted by the arrows of the castle guard, the beast apparently became frightened and flew away."

"Peripheral damage?" the king said.

"Lady Lilac is in her rooms being treated for general hysteria, repeated fainting, and intermittent shrieking fits. Also, in their rush to attain safety, two members of the court fell down a flight of stairs. One bloodied his nose."

Meg's eyes fell on Lord Fredrick the Thin. Although the man was holding an elaborately embroidered green-

and-purple handkerchief to his nose, he still managed to glare at her.

"So, daughter," the king said. "What do you intend to do about the havoc your unsuitable charge has wreaked on our kingdom?"

Meg knew the right answer, and it wasn't what she was thinking, which was: Poor Laddy! I have to go and find him! Instead she applied her lessons in statesmanship and said, "I am *very* sorry. Of course, I must see to replacing our flag and ensuring that Laddy does no further damage."

King Stromgard looked ever-so-slightly mollified.

Prime Minister Garald spoke up, earnest as always. "Princess, when you say you plan to replace the flag, I assume you mean you will embroider a new one. That seems fitting."

The king and queen exchanged glances. The only thing worse than Meg's magic was her embroidery. "Great-great-grandmother Ameliana was a queen, while I am merely a princess," Meg pointed out. "Surely it falls to my mother, who, by the way, embroiders really well, to create a new flag."

"Well said. Grand idea," the king put in hastily.

"My ladies and I will begin this very day," the queen said. "Perhaps we can even improve upon the design."

Meg stifled a grin. The old flag had been amazingly ugly.

With a few more promises and a couple of curtsies (Lady Evalines, she hoped), Meg managed to get out of the throne room. Before she did anything else, she knew she had to look for Laddy at Hookhorn Farm, which is where he was supposed to be, after all. Maybe once he'd pulled his stunt at the castle, he'd gone back to the farm in a snit. Somehow, Meg didn't think so, but she had to be sure. She took Dilly with her, not only for company, but so her mother wouldn't fuss. It was getting harder and harder for Meg to slip off by herself these days.

As they rode into the Witch's Wood, Dilly told Meg all about what had happened when the dragon flew over the castle. It seemed Nort had knocked Dilly down and bruised her shoulder.

"Why would he do that?" Meg asked.

Dilly let out a huff of air. "I have no idea. Addlepated guardsman."

"Addlepated apprentice guardsman," Meg remarked without malice.

"Right."

Nort had been very helpful a year ago, and Meg considered him one of her friends now. But Dilly didn't seem very happy with him. Meg changed the subject to her dragon. "Are you sure it was Laddy? Maybe everyone's wrong. Maybe it was some other dragon," she said, twitching Chloe's reins and leaning sideways to avoid some low-hanging branches.

"It was him," Dilly said.

Meg wished Dilly were wrong. After all, her father had warned her that keeping a dragon wasn't a good idea, but what was she supposed to do? Leave him out in the mountains? He'd nearly been killed by one of those awful princes. No, she had saved Laddy, and she was very glad she had, even if the flag of Greeve was in cinders because of it.

They were nearly to Gorba's cottage, so of course they had to stop in and say hello. Gorba was the witch of Witch's Wood. Gorba was cranky, but she wasn't wicked—not unless she was provoked, anyway. Today she sounded provoked. Meg and Dilly could hear her shouting as they rode up to the cottage. The two girls tethered their horses to the rickety front porch. Then Meg knocked on the door more tentatively than usual.

The door jerked open. Gorba's purple hair stormed about her head, matching the grimace on her lump-nosed face. "What do you want?" Her expression soft-ened a fraction when she saw them. "Oh, come in."

"Is something the matter?" Meg asked. The first time she'd seen Gorba's cottage, it had been filled with enchanted frogs that croaked and hopped and swam around in old basins and bathtubs. But they had all turned back to princes and gone on their way. The place seemed awfully quiet without them.

"It's this, this *creature!*" Gorba spat, leading them into the cottage. There, sitting in a ladylike fashion in the middle of a rag rug, was a small gray kitten. The kitten stared back at them inscrutably, then licked one dainty paw.

"A kitten?" Meg and Dilly stepped closer.

"How sweet," Dilly cooed.

"Sweet? Ha!" Gorba said.

"Not sweet?" Meg ventured.

"Not one bit!" Gorba said. "It's always been frogs with me. Frogs listen, you know. Frogs do what they're told." She stamped across the room to glare at the kitten. "But Miss Mystery here does not."

"Listen, or do what she's told?" Meg asked.

"Neither!" growled Gorba. She flung herself down on the sofa, which was cozily printed with sprigs of hemlock. "I'm at my wits' end!"

The kitten, bored, sauntered off in the direction of Gorba's kitchen.

Gorba snarled on, sounding like a cat herself. "After the others left and then Howie—well, I needed a bit of company about the place, didn't I? And I thought, I'm a witch, aren't I? I'll get myself a nice little kitten!"

"She's a pretty thing," Meg said. Prettier than Howie, the frog Gorba had carried in her apron pocket until the terrible day he had died of old age. He was buried in the witch's herb garden under an algae-colored ceramic plaque that said *Howie, Beloved Frog Friend* in curly letters.

Gorba wasn't finished ranting about the kitten. "She's scratched my furniture and she's broken the china statuette of the Bogeyman my old mother left me, *and* she walks around here like she owns the place!"

"That's what cats do," Dilly dared to point out.

Gorba didn't seem to hear. She pointed one wrinkled finger at the new arrival. "I'll show *her*. I'll cast *such* a spell."

"I've heard magic doesn't work on cats," Meg said, trying not to smile. "They're a lot like witches that way."

Gorba gave Meg a look. "Watch it, young lady. Just because you're a princess doesn't mean you can be disrespectful!"

"Sorry, Gorba. We'll come back another time, won't we, Dilly?"

"We will," said Dilly. "Bye, Gorba." The two girls let themselves out, leaving the witch muttering on the sofa. They untied their horses, mounted up, and went on toward the farm. They waited a sensible two minutes before they started to giggle and then laugh and even guffaw. The horses were startled and a little offended by the way Meg and Dilly pitched about in their saddles. Dilly's nearly threw her off.

Meg and Dilly finally stopped laughing and got their horses calmed down. "It could be worse, you know," Meg said.

"How?" Dilly asked.

"She could have gotten a dragon."

3

HEN THEY REACHED THE FARM, JANNA CAME out to meet them. "If you're looking for your dragon, he's gone," she told them.

"He flew over the castle and caused a ruckus," Dilly said.

"Oh, dear," the farmer said. "Come in and tell me all about it."

Meg and Dilly left their horses happily cropping grass in Janna's pasture and went inside, hoping for scones.

It was biscuits today. They were hot and buttery, fresh out of the oven. Meg and Dilly sat down at the kitchen table with Janna and ate their fill, trying to tell her what had happened at the castle without talking with their mouths full. Between the two of them, they got the story out.

Janna leaned back, folding her hands over her aproned stomach. "He's been acting so strange these past few months."

"Strange how?" Dilly asked.

"Well, he used to be such a cheery little thing. But ever since he got too big for the kitchen, even a string of sausages didn't help him out of those moods of his. He just lay in one corner of the barn with the gold coin you gave him, snuffling and whimpering to himself. A regular pity festival, I must say."

"Anything else?" Meg said.

Janna thought. "The last few weeks, early in the morning, he did a lot of flying. I'd see him at it, soaring over the cow pastures in the first rays of the sun. He made a pretty picture, as if he were painting the clouds with his wings." Cam's sister sighed. "I had no idea he'd go over to the castle and cause trouble, though."

"And then fly away," Meg said.

"He was getting very big."

"Too big for the barn?" Dilly asked.

"No. But he was restless. That made him too big for the barn, if you see what I mean."

"He couldn't stay there anymore," Meg said. She thought she knew how Laddy felt. She was feeling too big for the castle herself. She wished she could buzz the castle and fly away like Laddy. Meg smiled to herself. Of course, she might not have wings, but she had feet. She had four feet, actually, thanks to her horse, Chloe. And now, she was beginning to see, Meg had the best thing of all: a reason to go.

Meg soon convinced Nort and Dilly to go a-questing. She would have invited her friend Cam, but he'd made it clear he didn't particularly like adventures, so she left well enough alone. Fortunately, Lex agreed to go with her, too. The young wizard thought he could use one of Laddy's scales to cast a spell for finding Meg's lost dragon. What was more, Meg suspected her mother's usual worries would be calmed once she heard that Lex was willing to act as a sort of magical bodyguard to her daughter. And Meg was right.

Last of all, she approached her father, with her mother prudently in tow. To Meg's relief, King Stromgard approved of her going on a quest to search for Laddy. But he didn't approve of her going with just three friends, even if one of them was Lex. "The boy could fall asleep or wander off, and then where would you be, eh?"

"But—" Meg started to say.

"No daughter of mine goes anywhere in this kingdom with fewer than thirty guardsmen!" the king announced, sounding as if he were in the throne room instead of in his study, surrounded by bookcases and stodgy family portraits.

Meg refrained from pointing out that she'd been to Janna's farm yesterday with only Dilly for company.

"Now, dear, perhaps twenty guardsmen might suffice," the queen told her husband.

"Pomp and circumstance, Istilda, pomp and circumstance!" said the king.

Meg wasn't sure what this had to do with anything, but thirty guardsmen? Her quest wasn't turning out to be much of a quest, and she hadn't even *left* yet. Next her father would be demanding she dress up for the journey.

"And she'll wear her best court dress at all times," the king told the queen, as if on cue. "Can't have the populace thinking my daughter wears rags, can we?"

"Even to bed?" Meg asked, trying to remind them she was in the room.

"Silk jammies," the queen said automatically, and for a moment Meg was afraid her mother would take her father's side on this one. But Istilda wasn't finished. "Dear, we *have* been letting her study swordplay."

"Just in case," the king said, swirling one hand. "Really just for show."

"Or for palace coups," Meg said hopefully.

"Right. Palace coups." The king swept on. "This will be a royal processional, my dear, can't you see that?"

The queen cocked her head to one side. "It's more of a quiet affair. Ten guardsmen, riding skirts for our daughter, and don't forget the wizard."

King Stromgard frowned at his wife, but only a little. "Fifteen guardsmen."

"Twelve," countered the queen.

Meg had the good sense to hold her tongue during these deliberations.

"Fourteen," her father said.

"Nine."

"Ten!"

"Very well," said the queen. "Ten guardsmen. Two servants. And a lady-in-waiting and a wizard, of course."

"Of course," the king said. He turned a paternal eye on Meg. "Erm. You might want to take that scarf of yours. Just in case."

"Yes, Father," Meg said in her best dutiful voice. The magic scarf, which had been a gift from Gorba, was already lying on her bed waiting to be packed. And snoring just a little, the miniature lashes of its dozens of tiny closed eyes quivering. The thing was so sweet when it was asleep, Meg found it easy to forget how hard her scarf could bite when it got upset, or how loud it could shriek. On the bright side, it tended to get upset with Meg's enemies. She grinned as she left her father's study.

A day later, Meg had stopped grinning. Leaving the castle wasn't easy, even with the king's permission. The queen wanted Meg to take a carriage. A *carriage*! Meg was appalled. She was quite sure that heroes never rode off in carriages, especially not purple carriages lavishly trimmed with gilt curlicues. Had Great-great-grandmother Ameliana designed the carriage, too? Anyway, Meg wanted to ride a horse. After a very long conversation (not an argument—the queen *never* argued), Meg's mother finally consented to let Meg go on horseback, but only if she wore some extremely elegant riding skirts and let the guardsmen bring a wagon along for the luggage and tents and supplies. Meg secretly planned to bring sensible clothes to put on once she was well away from the castle.

Another day passed, with more preparations and details and deliberations than Meg could have ever imagined. She was starting to feel as if she would never begin her quest at all, that Laddy would be so far away she would never find him again. But finally the morning came when Meg and her companions were supposed to leave the castle. Meg went down to the courtyard, hoping for some sign that her quest was really taking place. She was pleased to find that several of her father's guardsmen had already led out their horses and were busy checking their saddlebags and gear. "Good morning," Meg called. The men smiled and greeted her in return. Ever since she had started studying swordplay, the guardsmen had been more inclined to treat her like a person instead of a princess. She knew a few of them by name—the old, grouchy one was Bumberson, the very handsome one was Frist, and the big blond boy with the quiet ways was Crobbs.

Then there were the two servants. Since Dilly was going, Meg had contrived to leave her rather useless maid behind. Instead, one man was being sent to cook, while another would drive the wagon and help with the camp. At first Meg barely spared the wagon driver a glance, but then her eyes were drawn back to him. He was wearing a straw hat, but something about him . . . *Cam?* Was that Cam?

Meg marched across the courtyard to the wagon, which was beginning to fill up with bags and boxes. "Cam?"

The wagon driver turned around from loading the wagon. "Good morning, Meg."

"What are you doing here?"

Cam shrugged. "I'm going to drive the wagon."

"But I thought—what about your vegetables?"

"They'll keep." This from the boy who lay awake nights worrying about whether his bean vines had caught a cold.

"Huh. You told me you didn't want to go on a quest. No adventures for you, you said."

Cam smiled faintly. "True enough."

"It's not that I'm not glad to see you, but did you change your mind?" Meg didn't think her old friend had changed that much over the last year. Janna's brother was still brown with the sun, his hair the color of freshly turned dirt. He still spent most of his waking hours thinking about vegetables. Only now he wasn't just the gardener's boy—he was an assistant gardener.

"No. Don't like adventures much." Cam was also sounding more and more like Tob, the chief gardener.

Tob was practically a plant, Meg thought. Or an old tree, gnarled and silent.

"Then why are you coming?" Meg asked, knowing even as she said it that she sounded ungracious.

"*Someone's* got to keep you out of trouble."

Meg had expected her parents to worry about her, and maybe Master Zolis, but Cam, too? Didn't anyone think she was capable of handling herself if she ventured more than twenty feet from home? All Meg could think of to say to Cam was "Hmph!" She stalked back into the castle to see if anyone else was ready. Unfortunately, she discovered that her mother was having second thoughts about the whole thing. Meg escaped back outside, wishing Lex would show up.

Lex was not a very complicated person. Take one dose of powerful magic and a cup of hot chocolate, then add the personality of a puppy, and that was Lex. It was hard to believe when you saw him that, with the exception of one very old wizard on the Isle of Skape, Meg's friend was said to be the best wizard in the known kingdoms. Of course, it was also hard to believe that a wizard would be named Lex. But that wasn't really his name at all—he had informed her that wizards kept their true names a secret. Meg had long ago given up guessing what Lex's name must be.

When Lex did finally arrive, he zoomed through the gates on what appeared to be a magic carpet. The gate guards ran into the courtyard after him, shouting. Meg emerged from her hiding place and waved both her arms. "Lex! Over here!" At which point he crash-landed two inches in front of her.

Meg was too pleased to be bothered about a mere brush with death. "I thought you got rid of your magic carpet!"

Lex stood up, coughing and slapping dust from his black clothes. His rooster's comb of red hair was even more rumpled than usual. "I bought a new one from a mail-order catalog. Well, it's used, actually. The catalog said the previous owner was an elderly wizard who only took it out on Sunday evenings." He lowered his shaggy brows. "But I'm not so sure. It's kind of unpredictable."

Meg felt her scarf loosen from her shoulders and float away. It circled the magic carpet, which lifted itself from the stones of the courtyard and circled, too, creating a kind of figure-eight effect. The scarf waved its deep blue fringes. Meg couldn't tell if it was threatening the newcomer or welcoming it, since she didn't speak cloth.

Lex tipped his chin toward the guardsmen and the horses and the wagon. "It's a lot of bother, isn't it?"

"Too much," Meg agreed glumly. Then she brightened, struck by an idea. "We could just take the carpet and hunt for Laddy!" She examined the carpet again. It was dark green, covered with mysterious markings in deep rose and gold. More important, it was big enough to carry two or three people without any trouble.

The young wizard was shaking his head. "I told you, it's unpredictable."

Meg's scarf flew back to her shoulders, apparently sulking.

"What do you mean, unpredictable?"

"I've taken the rug out a couple of times: around Crown, over to see Gorba, and across the Dreadful Moor." Lex sighed. "It got cranky and dropped me in the swamp. I had to walk clear home."

The rug ought to get along well with Meg's magic scarf, then. She never knew quite what the scarf would do. It gave a whole new meaning to the word "flighty." Still, Meg's hopes for an easy answer were definitely dashed. "So why did you bring the carpet at all?"

Lex looked sheepish.

"To make a grand entrance?" Meg guessed.

The young wizard smiled. "Always."

4

UARD CAPTAIN HANAK INTRODUCED MEG AND Lex to Lieutenant Staunton, who would be leading Meg's escort. The lieutenant looked as if he polished his hair with the same stuff he used to polish his boots. Staunton was so eager and formal and *blinky* that Meg knew she was in for a rough time. Or too smooth of a time, to be precise. Meg could picture herself facing a big purple monster, sword heroically in hand, and then Staunton would tap her on the shoulder, clear his throat, and say, "Now, Princess, you really *must* let me take care of that for you."

Of course, all she said was, "It's so nice to meet you." Statesmanship again. Meg swore silently to herself that if things got bad enough, she was going to find something a little less statesmanlike to do about it. For the moment, though, she was determined to grit her teeth and get out of the castle.

Introductions over, Hanak asked how they planned to find the dragon.

"Lex has a spell," Meg told the guard captain.

Lex held up a thin coin-sized object that shimmered red and gold in the sun.

Hanak peered at the jewel-like object. "Is that a dragon's scale?"

"One of Laddy's, to be exact," Lex said.

"Laddy?" Staunton repeated.

"The dragon's name is Laddy," Meg told the lieutenant.

"I see," Staunton said stiffly.

Lex continued his explanation. "I can use this scale to find the nearest place the dragon touched down. And that's south."

"The creature isn't likely to be there still," Hanak observed.

"No," said Lex, "so *then* we go to the next spot. And the next. Like visiting towns along a road. Until eventually he stays put . . ."

". . . and we catch up with him," Meg concluded.

"Good," Hanak said, satisfied. "Princess Margaret, I'm sure you understand that Lieutenant Staunton and his men will protect you on your journey."

"Of course." Meg made herself smile at Lieutenant Staunton. "How nice."

"Therefore," Hanak continued ominously, "though I see you're carrying your sword, I would very much appreciate it if you would refrain from fighting."

"But what if—" Meg began, unconsciously reaching for her sword.

"*And* from haring off into the wilderness unaccompanied by your guards."

Meg sighed. It was going to be like that, was it? She wasn't just being guarded against outside threats; she was being guarded against her own supposedly foolish ways. She winced, picturing the conversation the guard captain must have had with her father. "Yes, Captain Hanak. I understand."

Hanak bared his teeth in his own version of a smile. "Very good. If you'll excuse us . . ."

"Princess," Staunton said with a half-bow.

Meg nodded regally, but as soon as Hanak and Staunton went off to finish their preparations, she scowled.

"It won't be that bad," Lex told her.

"*We'll see,*" Meg said, feeling nearly as ominous as Hanak. If Lex weren't coming along, her parents wouldn't even have let her go, and now they had assigned her an official minder—one who was plainly determined to keep her from having any actual adventures.

Not quite an hour later, the company of questers really did leave. The king and queen came out to see them off, along with pretty much everyone else in the castle. "Now, daughter," said King Stromgard, "make us proud."

"Yes, Father."

"Did you remember your handkerchief?" Queen Istilda asked.

Meg managed to produce a handkerchief, and it was even still white.

"Take mine as well." The queen gave Meg her own handkerchief.

"Now, don't get out of sight of your guardsmen," said the king.

"Yes, Father."

The king turned to Staunton. "You'll take good care of my girl, won't you, Lieutenant?"

"My men and I will defend her to the death," the man responded.

The queen blanched. "Surely not death!"

"Bandits, swamp ghosts, nefarious wanderers, ancient evils." The king ticked things off on his fingers. "And don't let any dragons eat you. Not even that red-and-gold beast of yours."

Meg started to protest that Laddy would never eat *anyone*, then decided this last bit must be a joke. "Yes, Father." Meg hoped the king was finished, but he wasn't.

"Lex?" King Stromgard said, giving the wizard a look.

"I'll protect her, too, Sire," Lex promised. "But you left out a few things. What about cursed graves, witches (not Gorba, the other kind), and ordinary dangers like wolves and lions, also falling rocks and sudden storms?"

"Quite right," said Stromgard. "Watch out for those, too."

"I think I'll just go lie down," the queen said faintly. "Goodbye, dear."

"Goodbye, Mother. Don't worry, I'll be fine. Goodbye, Father!" Meg said. And they started out of the courtyard at last. The castle folk let out a cheer. Meg's heart lifted despite her worries. There was something exhilarating about the idea of *setting off*. Guardsmen and fussy fathers aside, Meg was finally going on a quest.

The traveling party made a modest yet noticeable procession. First came Staunton, resembling a statue called *Heroic Guardsman on Horseback*. Next came four slightly less heroic-looking guardsmen, including Nort. After that came Meg herself, wearing her magic scarf, with Dilly and Lex on either side of her. Behind them came the wagon, with Cam driving it and the cook sitting beside him. Five more guardsmen brought up the rear.

Meg looked sideways at Lex. She had already asked him if he would help her with her magic during the journey, but he hadn't really answered. She brought it up again as they began to canter past the city of Crown. "Lex, when we camp for the night, why don't I do a little spell, and then you can sort of critique it."

Dilly snorted. "*Little* spell?"

"Some of my spells are little!"

Lex appeared to be concentrating on his horseback riding, something he certainly needed to do, since the horse kept sneering at the wizard over its shoulder. It was a black horse. Lex had insisted. The horse went with his black clothes, which he wore in order to look suitably dire.

"Lex?" Meg repeated.

"Well, perhaps," he said. "You never know, with magic."

"That's just it!" Meg cried. "With my spells, you never know!"

"Meg," Dilly said, "everyone in the castle has heard of your spells."

"Everyone in Greeve," said Lex.

"Hey!" Meg said, objecting on general principle.

"There was the purple sludge that made everybody itch," Dilly said.

"So?"

"And the chair cushions that flew around the room," Dilly added.

"Yes, but—"

"And that time the autumn banquet turned to dirt."

"Well, *obviously* what I need is a good tutor. Like Lex," Meg exclaimed.

"I'll think about it," Lex said. "Is that farmer there carrying hen's eggs or duck eggs?"

It was a clear signal that this particular conversation

was at an end. But Meg planned to pester Lex again later. For now she focused on the sky, which was the perfect shade of blue, and on the crowds of travelers sharing the road with Meg and her companions: merchants and tradesmen and farmers and families, all dressed up and going to Crown for market day. Many of the people she passed smiled and waved, and Meg waved back. Once she even saw a band of players, their cart painted with vines and flowers. Meg wished briefly she could turn aside and watch the play, but then, she had a dragon to find.

Meg wasn't sure what she would do when she found Laddy. Talk to him, ask him what was wrong—she owed him a grownup name, for one thing. As she and Chloe clopped along, Meg tried to think of a name for Laddy that would be sufficiently grand without being gruesome. For example, Deathdealer seemed dragonish, but might give Laddy the wrong idea. It was really more suited to a warrior's magic sword, come to think of it. Dreadbreath? That reminded her of Lord Gatchen, whose breath was so bad people were always offering him mints or veering away from him at royal balls. Vermilion? Meg's dragon was partly red, after all. But that one sounded slimy to her, like an evil emperor or something. Goldenwing? Too pretentious, the kind of name you heard in a bad ballad. Meg frowned. "Lex, what would be a good name for a dragon? Dilly, do you have any ideas?"

"What's wrong with Laddy?" Dilly asked.

"Just help me think," Meg said. "I want a *grand* name for him."

So Dilly thought of Errol, but Meg said that was too human, and Lex thought of Gariloon, but Dilly said that was too frivolous, and Meg suggested Soarer, but Lex and Dilly both laughed because it sounded like "sorer." They ended up talking about how Lex should have taken riding lessons before they left, a topic which arose shortly after Lex's horse threw him in a ditch and two guardsmen had to fetch him out.

It wasn't that easy, naming a dragon.

As Meg and her party traveled farther south, they passed fewer people. The road began to seem endlessly the same, winding through rolling farmland, meandering between fields of barley and wheat. It was a great relief when they finally came to a small farm and Lex said, "Here! Laddy stopped here!"

At first they didn't see anything amiss. Meg and Dilly and Lex left their horses with a few of the guardsmen and approached the farmhouse door. The farmhouse was white with black shutters, but the door was bright red. To one side of the porch, an ancient dog rose up and gave a single huffing bark before subsiding.

Suddenly Lieutenant Staunton was stepping in front of Meg with a reproving look. "I'll just make sure every-thing's all right, Princess Margaret," he said, exactly as she had suspected he would. Lieutenant Staunton walked up the porch steps, but before he could knock, the door swung open, revealing the farmer and, peering around him, his wife.

"Good day, good people," Staunton said.

Meg managed not to laugh. *Good day, good people?*

"Who are you?" the farmer asked mildly. He had a droopy kind of face and his voice was deep.

"We represent the king," Staunton said in ceremonial tones. "We're wondering if you might have seen a dragon in the last few days."

The farmwife shoved past her man, easy to do since she was twice as wide as he was, round and outraged. "We most certainly have! That horrible creature frightened the chickens and attacked our smokehouse!" Her rust-colored curls bobbed when she talked.

"Can we see?" Meg asked.

The farmwife looked past Staunton at her. "It's out back, missy."

Staunton began to protest, probably about Meg being addressed as "missy," but Lex and Meg and Dilly were already walking toward the side of the house, the farmer and his wife right behind them, so Staunton gave up and merely came along. Cam had gotten down from the supply wagon, and he sauntered after them, too.

When they reached the smokehouse, Meg and the others could see that what used to be a small brick building was now half of a small brick building. One wall and the door had been torn off, and there seemed to have

been rather more fire than a smokehouse would normally have, outside as well as in.

"I don't suppose you had any sausages in there?" Meg
asked.

The farmer opened his mouth to answer, but his
wife spoke first. "Oh, it was *full* of sausages," she said.
"We were to take them to market in a fortnight, and now
what? The greedy creature gobbled them down!"

Cam idly picked up a charred brick.

"All red and gold it was," the farmer said in his deep
voice. "Never knew dragons were fond of sausages."

"We thought the monster would start on us next, but
it flew off instead," the woman said.

"Now, Teffie, you're not a princess," said the farmer.
"Dragons are partial to princesses."

"He wouldn't have eaten you!" Meg protested.

Everyone looked at her. "He?" the farmwife said
sharply. "What makes you think the beast's a male?"

"He's my dragon," Meg said, and flushed. "Sort of.
We're trying to find him before he does any more harm."

Lieutenant Staunton cleared his throat and tried to
take charge. "This is Her Royal Highness Princess Margaret. We are accompanying her in pursuit of the missing
animal."

"Then you'll be paying us for the damage," the
farmer said. "Those sausages would have brought us
more than—"

His wife interrupted. "Two hundred blenns."

The farmer seemed surprised. The woman rushed on. "And it will cost us four hundred blenns to rebuild the smokehouse."

Meg looked at Lieutenant Staunton. Her father had given her money for the journey, but she assumed Staunton had more to buy supplies along the way. She hadn't thought about having to pay for Laddy's misdeeds in actual coin. Six hundred blenns was a small fortune!

But Cam said genially, "You can't be thinking of rebuilding your smokehouse with gold bricks. And the sausages must have been made of diamond."

On hearing this, Lieutenant Staunton felt obligated to announce, "Defrauding the crown is an offense punishable by—"

"Lieutenant," Meg said. "Let Cam speak."

The farmwife glowered. "What about mental anguish? I've had nightmares ever since that dragon came. My nerves are a disaster, aren't they, Ogget?" She put out her hands and shook them a bit, trying to make them look like they were trembling.

The farmer, Ogget, nodded uncomfortably.

Cam addressed the farmer. "We'll give you fifty blenns for the sausages, a hundred twenty-five for the smokehouse, and another twenty-five for your wife's nerves." Cam grinned. "You could buy her a few new dresses, I'm thinking."

The farmer smiled.

"Ogget!" the woman shrieked. "You will not accept such a poor offer. My nerves are worth at least fifty!"

"Come on, dearheart," the farmer said, taking his wife by the arm. "I'm thinking you should offer the royal party a bit of refreshment while they count out the money." He led her back to the farmhouse, and her protesting voice faded away.

5

NOTHING ELSE HAPPENED THAT DAY. MEG WAS beginning to hope they'd run into something from her father and Lex's list of dangers by the time they stopped to camp for the night. Then she found out no one would let her help put the tents up or cook dinner or anything. She tramped around poking the tip of her sword into rabbit holes till Dilly told her to stop. "You'll wreck it, and for what? It's not like you're going to stab a rabbit."

"Stab a rabbit? I'd like to stab something," Meg said crossly.

But Cam was calling to Dilly, and Dilly went off, leaving Meg to entertain herself. Everybody was rushing around usefully except for Meg. Even her scarf seemed busy, hovering over the tents the guards were trying to put up, probably making a nuisance of itself. She noticed that Lex was talking with Staunton. Meg made a point of avoiding Staunton whenever possible. The fact that Lex was fraternizing with the enemy didn't improve Meg's mood.

That left Nort, who was doing something at the back of the supply wagon. Meg walked over to join him. But when she got there, Nort hurriedly pulled a heavy length of canvas over a pile of metal and looked up guiltily.

"What is that?" Meg asked.

Nort stepped away from the wagon. "Nothing. I was supposed to fetch a tool for the lieutenant, but I couldn't find it."

From the expression on his face, Meg was pretty sure he was lying. "I could help you," she offered, just to see what he would say.

Nort shook his head a little wildly. "No, no, that's fine. I have other things to do. I'll ask Lieutenant Staunton about it next time I see him."

Something was up. Meg looked across the flat, grassy area a short distance from the road that they'd chosen for their campsite. Cam and Dilly had built a fire and were helping the cook. Lieutenant Staunton had finished talking to Lex and was giving the guards orders now. "He's over there," Meg said, pointing.

"Um, thanks," Nort said, but he didn't leave.

After a few seconds, Meg realized he was waiting for her to leave first. "You're welcome." She forced herself to walk away, knowing that as soon as she got half a chance, she was going to sneak back and figure out what it was that Nort didn't want her to see.

Unfortunately, Nort stayed within sight of Meg all through dinner and afterward, too. Meg finally had to give up and go to bed. She was sharing her tent with Dilly, though, and after they'd rearranged their bedrolls a bit, she whispered to Dilly about what she had seen.

"It's probably nothing," Dilly said too loudly. "Nort's a gugglehead."

"Shh! People can hear anything we say in here." Meg paused, trying to decide how to convince Dilly that this was important. "I have to find out what it was. I want to be sure."

"Maybe he's hidden it," Dilly said in a much softer voice.

"We only have the one supply wagon," Meg argued. "The best he could have done is move it around a bit."

Dilly was silent for a moment. Then she said, "You're going to sneak out tonight and look, aren't you?"

"Right. And I have a job for you, too."

"What is it?"

"You have to distract the night sentry for me," Meg said.

"But if you have a candle, he'll still see you."

"I'll make do with moonlight."

"He'll hear you, then," Dilly warned.

"Not if I'm careful."

"This is what comes of you being bored," Dilly announced, not unkindly.

"This is what comes of something funny going on," Meg said.

Meg and Dilly had to wait until everyone else in the camp was abed. Tired as she was from riding Chloe for hours, Meg was determined not to fall asleep. Besides, she remembered something she'd been meaning to ask Dilly. "Did you and Nort have a quarrel?"

Dilly was silent.

"Dilly? It's just that whenever we talk about him, you sound like you're mad at him."

"He's been acting odd," Dilly said irritably.

"Odd how?"

"He avoids me for a week and then follows me around all day."

"Why?" Meg asked.

She could hear the shrug in Dilly's voice. "I don't know."

"Huh." Meg didn't, either.

"Eugenia thinks—oh, never mind."

Dilly had never bothered to care what Eugenia thought before. "What does Eugenia think?" Meg asked, amazed.

"She says Nort probably likes me."

"Well, of course he—oh, *likes* you."

"Exactly."

"Does he?"

"I don't know." Dilly sounded frustrated.

"Do you—um, what about you?"

"What *about* me?"

"Oh, nothing." Meg paused. "You don't have to be embarrassed, you know."

"I know," Dilly said in an embarrassed voice.

They were both quiet after that. Then Dilly slid down on her bedroll and fell asleep. Meg made herself stay sitting up. She considered what Dilly had said. Meg tried to picture Nort looking at Dilly *that* way and couldn't. She thought of all those princes who weren't coming around to court her and decided she was more glad than offended, no matter what her mother might say.

Which made her think just a little about Bain, a prince who was really a bandit. The last time she had seen him, he had given her the silver-hilted sword she carried. Meg wondered what he was doing now. She snorted. He was probably in love with some silly bandit girl. Or a silly reformed bandit girl, if Bain's sister, Alya the Bandit Queen, had followed through with her plans for the bandits to retire from banditing with all of the dragon gold they'd stolen.

Meg's mind wandered off in other directions. She listened to the night noises: Crickets, mostly. The cry of a night bird. Footsteps and snatches of talk. Little by little, the camp fell silent. Meg waited a bit longer; then she leaned over in the darkness of the tent and shook Dilly awake. Dilly made a snuffling noise and sat up. "What?" she croaked. "What happened?"

"Shh!" Meg said.

"What's going on?" Dilly whispered.

"I'm going to search the supply wagon, remember?"

Dilly finally woke up enough to remember. She and Meg put on their shoes and slipped out of the tent. A moment later, Dilly was sauntering across the camp, stretching her arms and yawning loudly, while Meg crept around behind the tents toward the supply wagon.

Meg looked up at the black sweep of sky festooned with stars and a languid moon. Her scarf glided by, looking like a piece of night sky itself, its blue-black darkness covered with tiny shining eyes like stars. Meg smiled to herself. She was out of her father's castle, and she was doing something exciting.

Meg could hear Dilly talking to the sentry, though she couldn't make out the words. She moved on, trying to roll her feet down each time she took a step. She'd worn thin leather slippers instead of boots because they would make less noise. She could feel every sharp little rock and twig she came across. Meg winced a few times, but she kept going, and pretty soon she was behind the wagon.

Only to discover that Cam was sleeping on top of the boxes and bales at the back of the wagon.

Meg retreated a step or two, trying to decide what to do. If Cam woke up, he'd probably make noise. He might even try to stop her. Still, she'd come too far to go back to bed without searching for whatever Nort had been trying to hide from her. At least Cam wasn't right at the *end* of the wagon. She could only hope Nort hadn't rearranged things, after all, and that Cam wasn't a light sleeper.

Meg reached for the canvas nearest her and lifted it as delicately as she could.

Cam didn't move.

She pulled it back slowly, slowly.

Then Cam's voice said quietly, "What are you doing, Meg?"

Meg let her breath out. She whispered, "I'm looking for something, and I don't want anyone to know."

"Except me," Cam said, sitting up.

"Except you, now that you've woken up."

Cam scrambled over the boxes and bales to the end of the wagon, managing to make a minimum of noise himself. "We haven't found any trouble, so you're going to make some?" he said. Though his tone was mild, his words weren't.

"It's not that," Meg explained. "Nort was acting sneaky, and I want to know why."

Cam considered this. "All right. I'll help you. But if the sentry comes—"

"He's talking with Dilly."

"Good idea. So what does this have to do with the supply wagon?"

"Nort tried to hide something from me this afternoon, here at the back of the wagon."

Cam climbed down to stand beside her. "Most of the wagon's filled with food supplies. The guardsmen put their weapons at the back. They told me to leave room."

"Did you watch?"

Cam thought about the morning when they'd loaded the wagon at the castle. "I was busy elsewhere. Meg, maybe you're imagining things."

"No, I'm not. Help me lift this."

They moved the canvas clear back. In the dim light, and by touching things carefully, they were able to identify a dozen crossbows with a matching supply of bolts, eight spears, and a couple of extra swords. There was something larger at the very bottom.

"What is it?" Meg whispered.

Cam felt the object. "It seems like a giant crossbow, designed to be shot by more than one person."

"For shooting what?"

"Monsters, city gates, giants . . ." Cam's voice trailed off in the darkness.

"Dragons," Meg hissed.

Cam was quiet for a long time. Then he said, "You might be wrong. You don't *know* it's meant to hurt Laddy."

"Oh, I know," Meg said, thinking grim thoughts

about Guard Captain Hanak and her father and Lieutenant Staunton, who must have planned this, all the while pretending they were helping Meg with her quest to bring Laddy home.

"What are you going to do?"

Meg had to admit that she was probably out of time with Dilly and the night sentry. "I'll get Lex to help me," Meg said. "I'll come back tomorrow night."

"Good night, Meg." Cam didn't sound very happy.

"Good night." Meg began the journey back to her tent.

Dilly met her there. "You took *forever!*" she said furiously.

"Shh!" Meg said again. She made Dilly wait till they were back in their bedrolls to hear about what she had found. "We have to do something," she concluded firmly.

Dilly argued with her, but only a little—and then they both fell asleep.

The next day, Meg restrained herself from stomping up to Lieutenant Staunton and telling him what a terrible person he was. She settled for the next-best thing, giving Nort a dirty look for not warning her what the lieutenant intended to do to Laddy. Nort seemed surprised and hurt, but Meg was already sweeping on to her breakfast of omelet and pan toast.

Once the company was on the road again, Meg talked

to Lex, though she let a little distance accumulate
between the guardsmen in front and Chloe before she
told the wizard what was going on. He didn't want to
believe the worst, either. "Now, Meg, it's probably just
for the perils of the journey."

Meg scoffed at this. "Nobody cares about Laddy but
me. And after what happened at the castle—"

"Well, you're right about that part," Lex said. Then
he had to stop talking to deal with his horse yet again.
The stallion took every sign of inattention on Lex's part
as his cue to cause trouble. It truly was a beautiful animal, tossing its black head and trying to climb up the
nearest embankment.

"Why don't you ask the guards for a *nice* horse?" Meg
asked. Lex shook his head stubbornly, wrestling with the
reins. Of course, a nice horse wouldn't be dramatic. It
might not even be black, which wouldn't do in the least
for the sinister wizard Lex liked to think that he was.
Meg returned to the matter at hand. "Anyway, I need
your help dealing with the thing. Tonight."

"Can't we just wait and see?"

"See what? Laddy's blood?"

"We could ask Nort."

"And give him a chance to guard it better? He may be
a friend, but he's a guardsman, too, and he *hid* it from
me," Meg said, outraged all over again. She collected
herself before she added carelessly, "I guess I could do a
spell on my own. If you're not going to help, I mean."

"What kind of spell?" Lex asked, instantly worried.

"I'll think of something," Meg said with a secret smile.

Soon enough, Lex was promising to meet her that night. See? she told herself. Statesmanship! She really should go on a diplomatic mission sometime. Looking for a lost dragon probably didn't count.

6

I T SEEMED UNLIKELY THAT DILLY COULD FOOL the sentry a second time. Besides, this was going to take longer. Meg concluded that Lex's first task would have to be putting the man to sleep. "Make it subtle," she reminded him that night in their new camp. "We want him to wake up thinking he dozed off, not that he was zapped by a spell."

"Got it," the wizard said. Now that he was past his initial resistance, he was quite pleased about slinking around at midnight. Meg had to tell him to keep his voice down, though. It was getting late, and Lex had come over to her and Dilly's tent, glad to share his endless supply of hot chocolate.

The three of them sat cozily in the tent, sipping hot chocolate and waiting for deep night. But whenever Meg thought about that monster of a weapon being aimed at Laddy, her thoughts burned like dragon fire.

Finally Meg thought it was late enough to get started. First she sent Lex out to deal with the night sentry. For such a chatty, bumbly boy, he was able to sneak astonishingly well. After a short while Lex reappeared. "All clear. He's asleep, dreaming fondly of his old mother and father back at home."

"Perfect!" Meg said. "Come on."

They walked softly through the camp. Cam was sitting on the wagon swinging his legs. He hopped down when they got there. "You're sure about this, Meg?"

"I'm not taking any chances."

Dilly stood watch in case anyone else woke up and interrupted them. It took Meg, Cam, and Lex working together to get the huge metal-and-wood crossbow out from under everything else without making a racket. At last they had it lying on the ground behind the wagon.

"It's actually a type of arbalest," Lex said conversationally.

"I don't care if it's your cousin Tilda," Meg retorted. "We have to get rid of it."

"Maybe we could just bury it," Cam suggested.

"No. They might find it. Lex?"

"Quiet, please," Lex said. The other conspirators fell silent, watching the wizard.

Lex's flair for drama seemed to be heightened on the stage provided by Meg's secrecy and the lateness of the hour. He swept his arms in half circles, chanting in a low voice.

There was a silence, followed by a noise like lips smacking and an explosion of darkness that blanked out a patch of stars for an instant. Then nothing. The crossbow—the arbalest—was gone.

"What did you do to it?" Cam asked.

"It's still there." Lex laughed. "I changed it to something else."

Meg peered down at the ground in the dim light. "What?"

"Dried grass. Twigs. Pebbles. Dirt."

"Very clever," Meg said admiringly.

"I know," said Lex.

At the sound of footsteps, they all jumped, but it was only Dilly. "Are you done? What did you do to it?"

Meg explained about Lex's spell. Dilly was impressed, causing Lex to preen the more. "We'd better get back," Meg said. And they slipped away to get some rest. Only Cam remained behind, and his good-nights were very subdued.

The loss of the weapon wasn't discovered for two more days. The questing company camped on the last of the grassy hills that evening. A thick forest filled the land ahead of them, to Meg's delight. There had been no sign of Laddy, and they'd long since left the farms behind. She was itching for something to happen.

Then again, a commotion over the missing arbalest wasn't what she had in mind. Meg was eating her dinner

when she saw the guards begin stalking around, confer-
ring with one another. It soon became clear that they
were searching the camp. Lieutenant Staunton looked
more perturbed than she'd ever seen him.

Some time later, the man approached her with a stiff
bow. Nort stood beside him, his lips pressed together.
"Your Highness," Lieutenant Staunton said, "we are
missing a valuable weapon."

Meg played dumb. "Has it been mislaid, then?"

"I'm afraid not. It has been stolen." Two other
guards approached with Cam between them. The lieutenant continued, "Our supplies master must have been
responsible. He was sleeping on the wagon each night,
guarding it."

Meg should have realized they'd blame Cam. No
wonder he hadn't seemed like himself since the night she
came looking for the crossbow. She rushed to fix things,
saying loudly, "Surely it could have been stolen during
the day?"

"Highly unlikely." Lieutenant Staunton's expression
changed. "Unless—Princess, do you know anything about
this?"

"She does!" Nort burst out. "She gave me a look!"

Meg made a puzzled face. "Everybody looks." She
gestured at Cam. "What could this man have done with a
weapon? Did you search his bags?"

The guards on either side of Cam tried to hide their

amusement. "It's far too large for that," Lieutenant Staunton explained.

Meg stood up, setting her unfinished dinner plate on her camp stool. "Then how could Cam have lifted the thing?" she said reasonably.

"*She* did it," Nort said. "To protect her dragon."

Meg resisted the urge to give him a far worse look. She had truly thought he was loyal to her.

"I'm sorry, Meg—Princess," Nort said miserably. "But you don't seem to understand how dangerous a dragon really is."

There was no point arguing with him, Meg told herself. Galling though it was, she knew Nort meant well.

Lieutenant Staunton narrowed his eyes. "I will ask again, Princess. Do you know anything about this?"

Meg was about to answer when she heard Lex's voice. "If you must know, *I* did it."

Lieutenant Staunton's face darkened as he turned to watch the young wizard approach. "The only reason you could have for doing such a thing is that you're an enemy spy!" All of the guardsmen took a step closer, although what they could possibly hope to do to Lex, Meg had no idea.

"Of course not," Lex said, startled. "I was just fiddling with the weapon when a spell went wrong, and I was too embarrassed to say."

Nort folded his arms. "His spells never go wrong."

"Hers do," someone said, but though Meg whipped her head around, she couldn't tell who had spoken.

Meg braced herself and took a step forward. "I haven't answered your question, Lieutenant Staunton. *I* stole the arbalest." Only it hardly seemed like stealing when the thing came straight from her father's armory.

Lex sputtered a bit, then stopped to listen. Dilly had come to stand beside him, her face filled with concern.

Lieutenant Staunton stared at Meg. "Why would you do such a thing?"

"To protect my dragon," Meg answered. "It appears I have been misled about the purpose of our journey."

"I see," Lieutenant Staunton said coldly. "And did it not occur to you that the weapon was meant to protect us against a great many dangers along the way?"

"Yes," Meg said. "Was it meant for Laddy, as well?"

Lieutenant Staunton said, "It was. But only if necessary, according to your father."

Meg knew, with angry triumph, that there was more to it than that. "And what about *you*? Was there any doubt in your mind that you would have to shoot my dragon?"

Lieutenant Staunton didn't answer for a moment. Then he said, with impressive formality, "No, there was not." He paused. "May I ask what you have done with my weapon?"

His weapon? Meg stood up straighter, wishing the man didn't tower over her. "It has been decomposed and is no longer available for your use."

"I see," the man said again, glancing at Lex. "Release the supplies master," Lieutenant Staunton said wearily. "He is not to be punished." The guards let go of Cam, who took a quick step back.

Meg made a move to leave, but Lieutenant Staunton wasn't done. "Wait, please. Princess Margaret, I may not be able to send you to your room, but I'll do the next-best thing. You will be kept under close guard for the remainder of our journey." He looked around at everyone's watchful faces. "In fact, I will give serious thought to turning back." With those words, Lieutenant Staunton walked away in the direction of his own tent.

The remaining guardsmen didn't seem quite so friendly now. Meg sighed and went to pick up her plate. She wasn't hungry anymore.

"You had to do it," Dilly said softly. "I *told* you Nort was a gugglehead."

"What is it about boys and dragons?" Meg asked with asperity. Dilly shrugged, knowing Meg really didn't expect an answer. Meg pictured Lieutenant Staunton meeting with her father and Captain Hanak, all three of them chortling and rubbing their hands together as they concocted their ruthless plan to shoot Laddy out of the sky. She scowled and took a bite of beef, forcing herself to finish her dinner.

Meg's quest wasn't nearly as pleasant the next day. Though Lieutenant Staunton had allowed them to travel on, he'd made it clear that Meg was in disgrace and that the company might turn back at any moment. He had assigned two guardsmen to ride on either side of Meg, so she was no longer able to laugh and talk with her friends along the way. Neither of the guardsmen was Nort, and neither seemed inclined to converse with Meg.

If she twisted around in her saddle, Meg could see Dilly's worried face and Lex's sympathetic one, but of course she had to face forward to keep Chloe on track. For the first hour she rode along dully, her eyes as much on Chloe's neck as on the road. It was only the thought of reaching the forest that kept her spirits from utter gloom. Perhaps they would find Laddy soon and everything would be all right. Then she remembered the spears and the crossbows. Laddy was still in danger from Staunton's men.

Last year when Prince Vantor had boastfully tried to kill Laddy, Meg had stolen the little dragon right out from under the man's nose and spirited him away. Some people thought Laddy was simply a souvenir of her adventures, but Meg knew better, though it was hard to put into words. Maybe she felt this way because Laddy's mother was dead, and Meg was the closest thing he had to a mother. Besides, Laddy had helped her fight the Battle of Hookhorn Farm and save her father's kingdom. He was worth fighting for now.

Meg's mouth tightened. It didn't matter if she was being treated like this. What mattered was keeping Laddy safe. It might even be better to go back home, to stay away from Laddy and hope for the best. But the thought made her heart sink. Meg couldn't go back till she had found out where Laddy had gone, and why. She lifted her head. Lieutenant Staunton or no Lieutenant Staunton, this was still her quest.

The day was long and hot. They were all relieved when they drew near to the edge of the forest, that first fringe of tall trees with its promise of shade. But there seemed to be something in the road, some kind of commotion at the front of the company. Everyone was stopping, and Meg craned her neck to see why.

At last word spread through the guardsmen, and Meg was told she was needed. She slid down from Chloe, hurrying to where Lieutenant Staunton waited with a frown on his face.

Beside him stood a peculiar little figure, an old man with bright, sparkling eyes and a gray beard down to his belly. The top of his head came up only to Lieutenant Staunton's shoulder, and not just because he was bent with age. The man's face had so many wrinkles there wasn't room for one more. He wore a cracked leather vest and a crooked felt hat that must have been green many years ago but had since turned a sort of brownish color. When he saw Meg he bowed, nearly falling over.

"This person wishes to speak with you," Lieutenant Staunton said in disapproving tones.

"Good day," the man said in a voice as creaky as his clothes. "Are you the royal young person on a quest?"

"Yes," Meg said, bewildered.

The man took out a little green notebook and a brass pen to make a note. "Oldest, middle, or youngest child of your parents?"

"Only," Meg said. "What are you writing?"

The man looked at her consideringly. "The bad luck of an eldest and the good luck of a youngest. Might cancel right out."

"Now, see here," Lieutenant Staunton began, but Meg was already talking. "Who *are* you?" she asked. "What do you want?" And, as an afterthought, "Have you by any chance seen a dragon?"

The old man tucked the notebook away, beaming. "First things first." He cleared his throat. "Ahem. I am old and alone and nigh unto death."

"Hardly," Lieutenant Staunton said.

The old man ignored him. "Could you spare a crust of bread, kind traveler?"

Meg was baffled, but she wasn't about to refuse a request that simple. Maybe the old man really was in trouble, though she wasn't sure what to make of the notebook or his odd questions. "I have a roll in my pocket. Will that help?"

The man nodded, pleased, and Meg gave him the roll, which was only a little squashed. He bit into it happily. Everyone waited while he ate the entire roll and then burped.

"*Now* will you answer my questions?" Meg said.

The old man bowed again. "*Now*, good Princess, I am going to help you get through the enchanted forest."

7

THERE FOLLOWED A THOROUGHLY ENJOYABLE interlude in which Lieutenant Staunton argued that the forest wasn't particularly enchanted that he knew of, which turned out to mean that the forest wasn't marked "enchanted" on the guardsman's map. Staunton also thought that the old man, whose name was Quorlock, only wanted a free lunch, also breakfast and dinner. Meg responded by acting on her strong belief that anything Lieutenant Staunton didn't want, she wanted.

Despite Meg's supposedly disgraced status, she was able to get her way, with the result that the old man joined the company as a guide.

Unfortunately, Quorlock hadn't seen Laddy. "But you will find, Princess, that those who enter the enchanted forest discover help therein."

"What kind of help?" Meg asked, interested.

"Magical, mysterious, and unexpected help," Quor-lock said, his eyes twinkling.

If Lieutenant Staunton hadn't been so proper, he would have rolled his own eyes. Instead he begrudgingly arranged for Quorlock to ride in Cam's wagon. At the front of the company, he might actually have been useful. As it was, Meg couldn't ask the old man any of her questions about the enchanted forest.

If there was ever a forest that deserved to be enchanted, it was this one. Oaks and maples, ash trees and beeches: the trees here were older and taller than the trees in the wood by the castle. Their heavy branches twisted out over the path, whispering greenly in the wind. Half-glimpsed animals, a low hum of insects, and the distant calls of birds, not to mention a sort of listening sensation, made Meg sure that at any moment she would see something new and magical.

She wasn't the only one who noticed, either. The guardsmen seemed more tense and alert than usual.

The tension broke a short while later when Lex fell off his horse again. The guardsmen pretended they weren't smiling, but Meg didn't bother to hide her grin. Not that Lex noticed. He tried to recover his dignity by using the occasion to confer with Lieutenant Staunton about Laddy's location—which suited Meg perfectly. She slipped off her horse and went back to talk with Dilly. The guardsmen glanced at each other, but there was no point in trying to stop her, so they didn't.

"Lex keeps telling jokes," Dilly said darkly.

"Oh no," Meg said. Lex and jokes didn't really mix.

Cam joined them. "Why isn't the old man up front, Meg? He told me he offered to guide us through the enchanted forest."

"One guess," Meg said.

"Lieutenant Staunton."

"Exactly." Lieutenant Staunton was arguing with Lex at the moment. Apparently Lex's magic showed that Laddy had touched down somewhere off to the south-west, and the path through the forest was still heading south. Lex wanted to leave the path or at least send a small party off to the southwest, but Lieutenant Staunton said they should keep going south and then veer off later.

To no one's surprise, Lieutenant Staunton won the argument. Lex wasn't wearing his customary smile as he joined his friends. "This could get interesting, you know," he told them.

"Why?" Meg asked.

Lex turned to look at the forest. "If it really is an enchanted forest, there will be surprises. Also rules, and I don't like rules very much."

"*Forest* rules?" Dilly said incredulously.

Lex nodded. "Stories matter in an enchanted forest. I just hope the forest doesn't get too fussy about it where we're concerned." With these cryptic remarks, the wizard walked to his horse and clambered on, still looking thoughtful.

None of the others knew what he meant, so Dilly changed the subject. "Maybe the lieutenant will forget about keeping you away from us now." She tried riding alongside Meg once Meg had returned to Chloe and Cam had gone back to the supply wagon. But Lieutenant Staunton hadn't forgotten. At his signal, the two guardsmen assigned to watch Meg flanked her, sending Dilly back to her place beside Lex. One of the men gave Meg an apologetic look as he did so, which made her feel the tiniest bit better. Not everyone was as coldhearted as Lieutenant Staunton.

It wasn't quite noon when Meg heard a cry up ahead. Something had crossed the path and was now rushing alongside them between the trees. Without hesitation, the guardsmen on either side of Meg whipped their horses around and followed it. Meg only saw the creature herself for a second, but it wasn't a sight anyone could forget: a great white stag with a forest of many-pronged antlers crowning its head. The creature looked like an animal, but its pelt was so pure a white that it practically glowed, whiter than anything Meg had ever seen, even snow.

Every single one of Meg's ten guardsmen raced after the stag, though Nort gave her a frantic backwards look as he left. Lex started to follow, too, but his horse didn't want him along and bucked harder than ever before. Lex promptly flew through the air again, hitting the ground hard as his bad-tempered horse disappeared into the forest after the others.

As for Cam, he was fighting to race the wagon between the trees, but there wasn't room. Cam's wagon hit the trunks with a wooden crunch, and he flipped off sideways into the underbrush.

Meg's startled scarf gave an earsplitting cry of alarm, leaping from her shoulders to rise high overhead. Lex's magic carpet hid behind a tree.

All of this took less than a minute to happen. Meg jumped off her horse, hoping Chloe wouldn't bolt. She had to see if Cam and Lex were hurt. Dilly was right behind her.

But even placid Chloe was snorting and rearing, apparently wanting to run after, or run with, the stag. She and Dilly's horse disappeared into the forest. Meg thought the camp cook was helping when he pulled the two carthorses loose from Cam's wrecked supply wagon. Instead he hopped on one of the horses and rushed off, with the other horse whinnying wildly after him.

Shaking her head, Meg turned her attention back to her two friends. Cam and Lex were more bruised than anything else, though Lex was a little wobbly and kept repeating, "Where's the stag?" Cam tried to slip away into the forest, but Dilly brought him back over and over again until he seemed to return to himself. Then he sheepishly set about examining the ruined wagon, while Lex lay propped up against a tree trunk, blinking as if it were a lot of work to move even his eyelashes.

"It's just the boys, isn't it?" Dilly whispered loudly to Meg. Meg nodded.

Behind her a voice said, "We really should be moving along." Meg looked over her shoulder. Quorlock stood there watching them, his expression more than a little smug.

"Did you do this?" Meg asked. He was the only one of the men who seemed to have been unaffected. Maybe he wasn't a man at all.

Quorlock laughed. "Now, how could I do such a thing?"

"Yes, how *could* you, exactly?" Dilly inquired.

Meg pursed her lips. "I'm guessing he didn't do it, but he knew it would happen."

"Or something like it," Quorlock said. "A quester's life isn't supposed to be easy, you know." He patted the nearest tree affectionately. "Dear old enchanted forest."

"Not so dear," Cam said glumly, staring in the direction the guardsmen had gone, chasing pell-mell after the magic stag.

"They'll be fine."

Meg wondered if Quorlock said that because he knew they would be, or because he didn't particularly care. "We should go search for them," she said.

"And abandon your quest?" Quorlock was outraged.

"Laddy can wait," Dilly remarked, frowning at the old man.

Quorlock shook his head, causing his long beard to swing from side to side. "They won't be easy to find, and they'll be harder still to stop. Let them finish the hunt, and they'll come back looking for you."

It sort of made sense. Meg hesitated only because she had just decided that Quorlock wasn't as trustworthy as she'd thought he was.

But then Lex seemed to come out of his daze. "Let's go find Laddy," the young wizard mumbled. It was the first thing he'd said in half an hour that *wasn't* about the stag.

Meg turned to Cam. He shrugged. "Why not?"

"All right," she said with a secret inner shiver of happiness. Lieutenant Staunton was gone, and she couldn't help feeling glad. What harm would it do the guardsmen to chase a stag for an hour or two? Meanwhile, Meg might just manage to have an adventure, uninterrupted by Staunton's supervision.

Dilly was still worried, though. "They'll be back soon, won't they?" she asked as the remaining travelers filled some shoulder packs Cam had found with food and blankets and water bags.

Meg remembered what Dilly had told her about Nort. "Are you worried about Nort?"

"Nort, Staunton, Frist, all of them," Dilly said

quickly. "That stag could have led them into a demon pit or something."

"This doesn't seem like a demon-pit kind of place to me," Meg said.

"Or something, then," Dilly said.

"Or something," Cam agreed.

Meg couldn't very well argue with that.

To the east, far across the forest, ten guardsmen and a breathless cook rode on and on through the enchanted forest, smashing through brambles and hurtling between trees, followed by four riderless horses, one of them a frenzied black stallion. Nort acquired a crown of leaves, nearly losing his entire head to a tree branch. Everything had happened so suddenly that he didn't have time to think. Then the stag filled his mind until nothing was left, not even his name. He wasn't aware of the other guardsmen riding beside him in the same mad haste to catch up with their quarry. Not that Nort knew what he would do if he caught the stag. He just knew he had to chase it—and then chase it some more.

There were five of them left, but Meg soon found herself wishing devoutly there were only four. Quorlock, now that he was walking along with her, took his duties as an enchanted forest guide far too seriously. The first sign of it came when he cried for them to stop.

"What? What is it?" Meg said so loudly that she

scared her scarf again. Truth be told, they were all a little nervous after the disappearance of the guardsmen, wondering what the forest might do next.

"An anthill!" Quorlock pointed down the path dramatically.

Sure enough, a large anthill teemed in the middle of the path. Meg and her friends exchanged mystified looks. "So?" Lex said.

"Maybe it's a nature lesson," Dilly whispered.

"Nature lesson?" Quorlock repeated, aghast.

"What about the anthill?" Meg asked.

"Princess, you must not step on the anthill."

"Bad luck, is it?" Cam ventured.

"If you are kind to the ants, they may be kind to you later," Quorlock said significantly.

"Huh." Meg came closer to the anthill and crouched to peer down at them. "These ants? Because we're probably never going to see these particular ants again."

"Perhaps not *these* ants so much as their relatives," the old man said, sounding a little confused himself.

Dilly must have guessed Lex was opening his mouth to make a joke about ants, uncles, and cousins because she said swiftly, "What good are ants, anyway?"

"Don't young people know *anything* these days?" Quorlock said, exasperated. "Ants can sort two kinds of grain out, for one thing."

"That sounds useful," Lex said in a placating voice.

Everyone murmured their agreement, though they

had no idea why. They walked around the anthill as care-fully as they could, though Lex's carpet seemed inclined to take a closer look, and he had to convince it to leave the ants alone.

Quorlock made another note in his little notebook. Then he started talking again. The old man tended to ramble on. Sometimes the stories he told were intrigu-ing, and the nature lessons—because there *did* end up being nature lessons—weren't too bad, either. Not at first.

Quorlock told them how garter snakes talked to each other with their scented tails. He warned them never to break a sapling for fear of offending the moss folk. He explained the difference between the samaras of the maple and the ash. He showed them the place where the red foxes danced by moonlight. He told them why the best spears were made of ash wood, but the most magical spears were made of the wood of the tree that grew in the very center of the enchanted forest. He also told them two stories about elves and one about chip-munks. It didn't take long for the rest of them to get tired of the sound of his rusty voice going on and on, and on and on still more.

8

THAT AFTERNOON MEG AND HER COMPANIONS came across a clearing with a few logs and rocks lying around and took advantage of the ready-made seating to eat their lunch of bread, dried meat, and cheese. While they ate, Cam and Lex began arguing about whether they should leave the path. Laddy was off to the southwest, but up until now the little company had kept to the path to make it easier for the missing guardsmen to find them when they came back. *If* they came back.

In the middle of the discussion, Meg heard a peeping noise in the grass. She got up from the log she'd been sitting on and searched until she discovered the source of the sound: a gawky bit of fluff and beak and clawed feet. "Poor thing," she said, picking up the baby bird gently. She looked straight overhead to see if she could spot the nest. Meg was pretty sure she could make out some sticks and clutter in the fork of two branches high above her.

"What is it?" Dilly asked.

"I found a baby bird."

Quorlock hurried over, beaming with pride. "*Very good*, Your Highness! Now you'll put it back in its nest, and when the time comes—well, we shall see."

"What will we see?" Cam asked.

Meg could feel the bird trembling in her cupped hands. It spoiled things to have Quorlock meddle, as if he'd invented her. She tried not to think about it, examining the tree trunk to figure out how hard it would be to climb. She envied her scarf, which floated lazily upward to see what Meg was looking at.

"I can do it," said Cam.

Lex wiped the crumbs from his mouth. "I could probably use a spell. Or my carpet."

Dilly, who was afraid of heights, crossed her arms. "Go right ahead."

When Quorlock was worried, the number of wrinkles on his face increased impossibly. "The princess has to do it with her own hands," he said with all the conviction of the very old and unpleasantly wise.

Well, she *had* found the bird. Meg didn't answer the old man, but she tucked the creature into her loosest pocket and said, "Cam, give me a boost, will you?" He obligingly helped her reach the first branch. Then she scrambled higher until she could shinny out onto a thick limb to the fork she'd targeted. The fork did cradle a nest. Inside of it, two more baby birds stretched their little necks, gaping greedily in hopes that Meg would ply them with worms. Instead she deposited their missing sibling into the nest and began her return journey.

When she got back down, Quorlock was still grinning and chuckling as if he had planned the whole thing.

"What? What are you so pleased about?" Meg demanded.

Quorlock raised his brows. "It's best if I don't say too much." This from a person who'd been talking nonstop for hours, Meg thought sourly.

"Are you going to tell us birds can be helpful, just like ants?" Cam said.

Quorlock turned a sharp eye on him. "No need to mock, young sir. Birds can also sort grain. They can act as messengers, they can bring things back from the sky— lots of handy things a bird can do. Assuming she owes you a favor."

The old man could tell they didn't believe him, so he got into a real snit, shutting his mouth for a good while as they continued on their way.

This was a relief to the other four travelers, who had taken to talking about WOM (Wise Old Man, pro- nounced in ironic tones) behind his back.

Nevertheless, Meg managed to rescue a fox with its leg in a trap, flip a gasping fish back into a forest pool, and save a mouse from a hawk before the day was over.

"How come I never get to rescue any animals?" Dilly asked plaintively.

"We could take turns," Cam said. Meg was pretty sure he was joking.

On hearing this, however, Quorlock was distressed enough to express his opinion again. "The princess is the quester, and she must accomplish a quester's tasks," he proclaimed.

Meg had to protest. "We're all questers," she said.

"Your dragon, your quest," Lex told her.

Of course, there were other things to distract Meg from Quorlock's strange remarks about her responsibilities. The fact was, the forest was acting more enchanted by the minute. On top of the highly coincidental series of animal rescues, there were little green eyes watching them from beneath various bushes.

"What *are* those?" Dilly asked.

"Pixies?" Meg said.

"Goblins," Lex suggested.

"I don't want to know," said Cam.

Meg's scarf wanted to know, though. It kept dashing under the bushes and then dragging itself back, looking annoyed. Apparently whatever was watching them was too fast for the scarf to catch.

Next an eerie song began riding the already eerie wind. The notes wrapped around their heads, slid into their ears, and refused to leave. "Do you think Lieutenant Staunton believes this is a magic forest yet?" Meg asked. Everybody laughed, even the old man.

Naturally, Quorlock cheered up just in time to talk their ears off when they stopped for the night. On the bright side, Meg finally got to help set up camp and build a fire. Quorlock kept a close eye on her the whole time, though, telling her what she was doing wrong, so it wasn't nearly as much fun as it should have been.

The next morning, Lex checked his Laddy spell, only to learn that the dragon had last touched down west of them. Lost guardsmen or no, it was time to leave the path. Besides, Meg pointed out, Quorlock could help them find their way even without the path.

The others looked dubious, but Quorlock smiled his wrinkly bearded smile. "Yes, Princess, that I can."

None of them was used to this much walking. Each of them had at least one blister, and Meg had three. "Don't you know any blister spells?" she asked Lex.

"I know spells for *causing* blisters. I'm not a healer, Meg," he said apologetically.

So they tromped onward, their feet hurting. After they'd traveled west for what seemed like forever, they sat down to rest by a small stream.

"We can refill our water bags here," Cam said.

"No we can't," Lex told them.

"Why not?" Meg asked, surprised.

But Quorlock answered before Lex could. "In an

enchanted forest, drinking from a stream is a dangerous thing to do."

"You might turn into an animal," Lex explained. Meg decided he must have studied up on enchanted forests at some point in his magical training.

"But if we run out of water," Cam said, "we'll have to take a chance."

Dilly turned to Quorlock and said accusingly, "If you're such a good guide, why can't you tell us if this stream is enchanted?"

"Sometimes the streams are safe, sometimes they're not," the old man said. "Keeps things lively around here."

Dilly gave up. "I'm not that thirsty."

"You can have some of my water," Meg told her.

In the end, they crossed the stream without refilling their water bags. But their water would only last another day. Unless they left the forest, they were going to have to drink from a stream soon, Meg thought.

Not long afterward, the five travelers reached a clearing and stood gawking upward. Finally Lex said, "This is it. This is where Laddy landed."

"It's a tower," Cam said unnecessarily.

Everyone looked at Meg.

"I hate towers," she said, just in case anybody had forgotten that only a year ago her father had sequestered her in one.

High above them, a head poked out of the window.

"Help?" a girl said, looking positively sweet and definitely imprisoned.

"Don't worry," Meg called. "We'll get you down!" Meg's face filled with indignation. "What is *wrong* with people? Why are they always putting girls in towers?"

"Only twice," Lex said, but Meg ignored him.

Then Quorlock stepped forward. He seemed upset for some reason. "Now, just a minute here. You can't go messing up stories and spells in this forest."

"Watch me," Meg said calmly. Apparently rescuing the girl was against those enchanted forest rules Lex had mentioned, but Meg didn't care one bit, and neither did her friends.

"Of course we have to get her down," Dilly said.

Quorlock flipped through his notebook as if that would help him stop them, but Meg had already forgotten him and was beginning to circle the tower. The others followed.

"No doors," Cam said when they had come back around.

Puzzled, they looked up at the girl again. "Who put you there?" Lex asked.

"My mother," the girl said. "When I was very small. She comes to visit me. Or—she used to. Something's wrong."

"How does she visit you without a door?" Dilly asked.

"We use my hair," the girl said.

"Hair?" Dilly repeated, mystified.

In answer, the girl started feeding a long, ropelike object out the window. It dropped down and down until Meg was astonished to see that it was a long blond braid.

"What is it for?" Lex said.

"My mother climbs up my braid," the girl said.

"Doesn't that hurt?" Meg asked.

"I anchor it up here on a hook," the girl explained. "My mother brings me food. But she hasn't come in days, and I've run out of food."

"We'll help you," Cam said. "What's your name?"

"Spinach," the girl replied.

"Spinach?" Dilly repeated. "Why are you named Spinach?"

"My mother liked spinach," the girl said. "That's what my mother says—the one I have now. My first mother went away."

There was a moment's silence in honor of Spinach's first mother. Then Meg thought to ask if the girl had seen a dragon.

"Yes," Spinach said eagerly. "How did you know?"

"Because we're trying to find him," said Lex.

"Did he frighten you?" Cam asked Spinach.

"At first he did. I hid under my bed. But then he was whining and poking his nose in the window, more like a puppy than a dragon."

"What did you do?" Dilly asked.

Spinach was really very pretty, with that delicate lily

look that princesses were supposed to have. That Meg didn't have, she thought ruefully as Spinach explained about Laddy. "I gave him a piece of bread, and he ate it. So then I scratched his nose. He liked that. But when he decided I wasn't going to give him any more bread, he got bored and flew away." Spinach paused. "I wish I could have gone with him," she said pointedly.

"You can come with us," Cam replied.

Getting Spinach down wasn't easy. Meg thought that Lex could use his magic carpet. The carpet didn't seem very cooperative, however, even after they had coaxed it over to the right spot. "Wish me luck," Lex said, eyeing the carpet as it quivered impatiently a handbreadth above the grass and dirt.

"I have some rope in my pack," Cam said, but everyone was watching Lex. The wizard acted like a bear tamer about to tame a bear. Or be tamed by the bear, Meg wasn't sure which.

"Now, come on, you," Lex announced. "We need to rescue a damsel in distress."

"I'm not distressed," Spinach told them. "Just hungry."

Lex pounced on the magic carpet, which sullenly bore his weight. "Up, please," Lex said. The carpet rose a few feet in the direction of the tower. Lex started to look hopeful. The carpet rose through the air more surely, bringing Lex closer to the window where Spinach waited expectantly. Lex was nearly there when the carpet swerved away suddenly, dove down, and flipped the wizard halfway across the meadow. Then it did the flying equivalent of a saunter, moving away toward the edge of the meadow, where the scarf appeared to be snickering.

Dilly helped Lex to his feet. "Are you all right?"

Lex coughed. "More or less." He shook his head. "Sorry, Meg. We'll have to think of something else."

"First the horse, now the carpet—none of your vehicles likes you," Meg said.

"The forest doesn't like *this*," Quorlock admonished them. "It won't let you."

But Cam stepped forward. "Let's keep it simple." He held out a coil of rope. Quorlock retreated to the other side of the clearing, his expression dour.

They ended up tying the rope to Spinach's braid so Spinach could pull the rope up. Then she tied the rope to the hook inside the tower instead of her braid.

The braid was actually kind of a problem. It kept tangling in the rope as Spinach tried to come down. Finally Cam climbed up the rope and helped Spinach sort herself out. He was awfully patient about it.

Dilly nudged Meg. "Look at those two."

Meg squinted. "Two what?"

Dilly laughed softly. "You just don't notice these things, do you, Meg?"

"What things?" Meg flushed. She liked to think she was observant, but it seemed spending time with the ladies-in-waiting had taught Dilly a whole new kind of observation.

"Never mind," Dilly told her as Cam and Spinach descended.

They had to redistribute things to empty out a pack so they could stuff Spinach's braid into it, otherwise the hair would have dragged along the forest floor behind the girl as they walked, catching on everything.

"Have you ever thought of cutting it off?" Meg asked cautiously, but Spinach seemed so shocked at the idea that Meg didn't say anything more about it. Meg wasn't sure what to think of this girl. She was sure of one thing, though, and that was that no one should be stuck in a tower.

9

IN ANOTHER PART OF THE ENCHANTED FOREST, ten guardsmen and a camp cook lay groaning in a heap. Nort lifted his head and stared around, bewildered. There were no horses in sight. Lieutenant Staunton seemed to be unconscious. Nort's heart sank. He was supposed to catch something, and he had failed. But he couldn't remember what it was. "The stag," somebody moaned, and Nort remembered. He sat up, which made his head hurt. They had been hunting the white stag. But now it was gone, and nothing mattered at all anymore. Nort frowned. There was something else—a castle? A king? Nort gasped as his mind filled up with knowing, like water pouring itself into a cup. "Get up, all of you!" he cried. "We've lost the princess!"

Meg thought Quorlock would stop complaining about Spinach now that the girl was actually out of the tower, but he seemed to get angrier and angrier. When Meg and her friends shouldered their packs to continue their journey, Quorlock stood there as if he had taken root.

"Aren't you coming?" Meg asked.

"You have to respect the enchanted forest," Quorlock said stubbornly. "Put her back."

"Spinach?" Meg said, amazed. "We just got her down."

"Getting her down is a job for a handsome prince!" Quorlock roared. "This is *not* her story!"

"Maybe it is," Lex remarked. "Maybe you think you know her story, and you're wrong."

Quorlock sputtered, then said again, "Put her back."

"Or what?" Meg asked. "You mean you won't come with us if we take Spinach?"

"That's right," the old man told them.

"Well then, thank you for all your help, but we're leaving now, and Spinach is, too. Goodbye."

"Goodbye," Meg's friends chorused, not disappointed in the least.

From the look on Quorlock's face, he couldn't believe they weren't going to obey him.

Meg and her companions began to walk away. Then Lex said, "There's one more thing." He stepped toward Quorlock. "Isn't there?"

"I don't know what you're talking about."

"Oh, I think you do," Lex said pleasantly. "Don't you

have a little gift for the quester, to speed her on her way and encourage her success?"

Quorlock crossed his arms. "She's not a very nice royal quester."

"How can you say that?" Dilly demanded. "She gave you bread and listened to all your stories and rescued a bunch of animals. She's a *very* nice quester."

Lex's eyes gleamed. "You accuse her of not following the rules, but you're about to break one?"

The old man made a harsh sound like a raven's croak. "Young people these days," he snapped, and he started digging around in various pockets.

Meg opened her mouth to ask Lex what was going on, but he was already explaining. "He's giving you a magical artifact, Meg. It's the way these things are done."

Come to think of it, Meg could remember reading stories like this. "Really? What kind of artifact?"

"Amulet, magic sword, invisibility cloak," Lex said, watching Quorlock closely. "Something like that."

Quorlock growled all the more, his long beard quivering with indignation, but he tried another pocket and finally fished out a small object. He glared at Lex before slapping the thing ungraciously into Meg's outstretched hand.

Meg inspected the object.

"What is it?" Spinach asked.

Cam leaned over to see. "A broken piece of china?"

"Hand-painted with roses," Dilly added sarcastically.

Meg looked up at Quorlock. "What does it do?"

"That, young quester, is for you to discover," Quorlock pronounced, and he grumped away into the enchanted forest.

Meg tilted the shard of china in her hand, hoping it would change into something more impressive.

Lex reached out to touch the china with one finger. He licked the finger, which sparkled for an instant. "It *is* magic," he said.

"Well, it must do something," Meg said. "We'll figure it out. But for now, let's get going."

With that, the five of them marched off to find the next place Laddy had touched down. Spinach trailed behind a little as she checked once more to make sure her entire yellow braid was tucked away in her pack. Then she caught up with the others and asked, "What are those green-eyed things under the bushes?"

Once Nort and the other guards had stopped feeling dazed and weak, they switched over to feeling embarrassed and angry at themselves. Lieutenant Staunton was the worst. They were finally able to rouse him and he proved able to walk a little, but he soon went into a dark mood, making pronouncements such as, "I have failed my monarch." They tried to reassure him in vain. It was only when somebody suggested that they really should go look for the missing princess that he seemed to recover a little of his crisp leadership style. Well, not so crisp, actually. The men straggled rather than marched, and nobody wanted to admit that they didn't know where they were in the slightest, let alone what had happened to their horses. All the guardsmen and the cook could do was to follow Staunton, hoping they would come across Princess Margaret and her friends. "That wizard is probably taking good care of her," Nort said, trying to be consoling, but for some reason this didn't make the lieutenant feel any better.

Spinach wanted to know about everything. "Why is your hair that color?" she asked Lex. "Why are you following a dragon?" she asked Meg. She pestered Cam to tell her about the castle of Greeve. She inquired why Dilly wasn't as skinny as Meg. Dilly flushed and avoided Spinach for a while after that one.

"It's like having Quorlock, only with questions instead of answers," Lex whispered to Meg, who knew exactly what he meant.

Late that afternoon, Meg's party came across another stream. "Oh good," Spinach said happily. "I'm thirsty!"

Meg opened her mouth to speak, but Lex beat her to it. "The water is dangerous."

"We don't know that for sure," Cam explained. "But we haven't wanted to take the chance."

"Is it poisonous?" Spinach asked, crestfallen.

"Worse," Lex said. "It might be magic."

"Might be?" Spinach repeated. "You mean bad magic? How can we tell? Does magic water sound funny, or taste funny, or does it act just like regular water?" She stepped closer to the stream, and the others followed. It looked ordinary enough, with pebbles and the occasional larger stone showing beneath clear tumbling water. Grasses and small bushes leaned over the banks as if they might fall in at any moment. "It seems fine to me," Spinach said longingly.

"I'll go first," Cam said.

"No, I will," Spinach insisted, and Meg decided maybe the girl with the endless braid wasn't so bad, after all.

Spinach knelt down beside the stream, scooping up water in her hands to drink it. "It tastes nice," she told them.

They waited a few minutes just to be sure, but Spinach didn't seem any different from before. Relieved, the others drank the water. They filled their water bags, too.

Cam came over to talk to Meg. "Do you want to keep going? I was thinking maybe we could camp here."

The sun was low in the sky. Not that they could see it, but the shadows were darker and the green leaves of the trees were dimmer now. Furthermore, everybody seemed to be walking more slowly. "This will do," Meg said.

They were too tired to bother with a campfire. Meg and her friends ate dried meat and increasingly odd-tasting cheese from their packs again. Lex had run out of hot chocolate, which Meg at one time would have said was impossible. There wasn't much food left, either. But Meg had worse things on her mind. She was getting more worried about the missing guardsmen—and feeling guilty on top of it for having been glad they were gone.

Meg wasn't the only one who was worried, either. "They're just lost, aren't they?" Dilly asked her.

"Who's lost?" Spinach asked. "Did you have more friends with you before you came to my tower? How many were there? Did you find them, like me, or bring them from home?" When she stopped to catch her breath, the others explained what had happened to their former companions. After that, they took turns asking Spinach questions about her life in the tower. Spinach seemed a little surprised not to be the one asking questions, but she told them as much as she could.

At last it was night and everybody fell asleep, worn out from walking for hours. Everybody except Meg. Her mind wandered here and there, until finally Meg concluded that she couldn't sleep at all. She got up to walk restlessly around their makeshift campground in the starlight. They hadn't posted a sentry, she realized suddenly. Lieutenant Staunton would not have approved.

Meg brightened as she thought of a way to banish Lieutenant Staunton from her mind, along with all of her other worrisome thoughts. She would practice her magic, just a small spell. Meg glanced at her sleeping companions. For some reason, they seemed to think she shouldn't ever do magic. Which was silly, because how was she going to get any better at it if she didn't practice?

Even so, Meg moved well away from her friends before she got started. At first she couldn't think of a spell she could do with the materials at hand, let alone one that might be easy to do in the dark. But the darkness reminded her of one of the first spells Master Torskelly had tried to teach her. Meg found a rock and began muttering the spell, which was supposed to make the rock glow.

She had only said a word or two when Meg heard a voice from behind her. "What are you doing?" Oh no, she thought. It *would* be Lex.

"Nothing. Go back to sleep."

The boy had a real nose for magic, unfortunately. "Was that a spell?" he demanded.

Meg didn't answer, which was pretty much an answer. Finally she said, "I couldn't sleep."

"Now, Meg," Lex said gently, "this place is full of strange magic. Who knows what the forest might do if it meets up with your magic?"

Meg was about to snap at him, but something poked Meg in the back and she yelped instead.

"Are you all right?" Lex asked, alarmed.

Meg had already recognized the source of the motion. "It's only my scarf," she said.

The scarf caught Meg by the hair and tugged. "What?" Meg asked.

"I think it wants you to go somewhere," Lex observed.

Not for the first time, Meg wished her scarf could talk. She started to walk after it, trying to see where it was going. She'd rather do that than quarrel with Lex about how bad she was at spellmaking.

"I'll come with you," Lex said.

"All right." Meg didn't know whether to be glad or envious that Lex didn't need any glowing rocks to make a light. He simply held up one hand, his palm shining. Meg concentrated on making her way between the shadowy trees and bushes, following the midnight-blue flitter of her scarf.

They had been walking for at least twenty minutes when the scarf stopped and hovered, pointing with one end, which seemed to have been designed for just that purpose. Meg and Lex saw that the scarf had led them to a cottage. More of a hut, really, though it was hard to see very far in the faint light from Lex's gleaming hand.

As they drew closer, they saw that the hut was leaning at an odd angle. It appeared to be made out of lizard skins, or even dragon skins, Meg thought, her heart lurching. But the skins, stretched over some kind of knobbly framework implying tree branches, were weathered as if they were ancient. They were black and gray and brown, too. Only one piece gleamed green in the light Lex cast on it.

"Should we go in?" Lex whispered.

Meg spared him a look. "You're not scared, are you?" Some bodyguard he was turning out to be, she thought wryly.

"Of course not!"

They approached the hut's ill-cut door together. Meg tried the handle, which stuck a bit. She pushed the door open slowly, and she and Lex went inside.

Though it wasn't nearly as nice as Gorba's, the hut was a witch's house. Meg could tell because of the snarling black cat, the noxious herbs hanging on the walls, and the shelf filled with malevolent-looking books. Also because of the dead witch on the bed.

10

A T FIRST MEG AND LEX DIDN'T KNOW SHE WAS
dead. They stumbled and shoved their way back
outside, whisper-shouting, "Did you see that?"
and "Hurry up!" But if the witch was merely sleeping,
their entrance hadn't wakened her. The only sound was
the mew of the cat. He had changed his mind almost
immediately in a catlike way, deciding to be friendly to
the newcomers—no doubt because they were alive, a useful sort of state to be in.

After a long pause during which absolutely nothing
happened, Meg and Lex made themselves go back into
the hut and get a better look at the witch. She lay atop the
rickety bed like a badly wrinkled statue. She wasn't moving. She wasn't breathing. Unless she was under some
astonishing new kind of spell, she was dead. She also
seemed sort of dried up, which might have explained
why the smell wasn't worse.

Nervously, Meg and Lex explored the hut. They weren't at all sure what they were looking for. Lex was the one to find it, though. "Come see," he told Meg softly, holding his glowing palm next to one of the rough shelves on the wall of the hut. There among the shrew skulls and dried mushrooms, between a jar marked *Orifices* and a metal box filled with wood shavings and who knows what else, was a picture in a pink frame. Inside the frame was a painting of Spinach—a few years younger, perhaps, but definitely Spinach. She was half curtsying in a fluffy blue dress, her braid done up in a towering triple crown of braids that was evidently meant to be fancy.

"Oh," Meg said. They both looked back over at the witch. "Maybe . . ."

"She's very old," Lex said.

"I always thought of witches as dying in horrendous battles or iron ovens or magical backlashes," Meg explained.

Lex grinned. "You would know something about magical backlashes."

"That's not funny." Meg tucked the portrait into her pocket. "Let's go."

The cat left through one of the back windows before they could bring him out the front door.

Just outside the edge of the enchanted forest, something was happening. From high overhead, a patch of sky rolled downward, re-forming itself improbably into the shape of a staircase. Then anyone who was listening could have heard the sound of giant footsteps descending ponderously. THUD. THUD. THUD. THUD. THUD.

Closer and closer the footsteps came, until finally two colossal feet reached the ground and stepped off the sky-stairs, crushing a couple of saplings that happened to be growing in what had suddenly become a treacherous spot. Three crows flew off squawking dramatically, as if on cue. But nobody was there to look up and up and farther up to see the giant's tremendous body, and to see higher still his gruff red beard followed by grouchy but not-at-all-stupid eyes.

Not yet.

Nort hung back to help Crobbs again as the men ahead of them called that they had found a stream and rushed down to the water to drink. Crobbs was only a few years older than Nort, but he was more than a head taller. If he hadn't been so dull and pleasant, with a smile always spread across his round face, Nort might have been jealous, since Nort had always wished he were a head taller and two years older than himself. And now Crobbs was acting a little funny—he had been ever since the guardsmen had recovered from the stag's enchantment. The big blond boy was prone to wandering off in the wrong direction. Nort wasn't sure if Crobbs had bumped his head or if the spell of the stag was lingering in the older boy's mind, but he had taken it upon himself to keep an eye on Crobbs so they wouldn't lose him in the forest.

If Nort hadn't been busy herding Crobbs for the fourth time that morning, he would have taken a drink from the stream, too. As it was, he and Crobbs were walking up behind the rest of the men when they saw something strange and dreadful happen. The other guardsmen and the cook, who had been wiping their wet mouths and laughing and talking, grew quiet, looking at each other with frightened eyes. Then one by one the nine men shrank, yelling until their yells were cut off as their bodies distorted into smaller shapes and fur sprouted across their hands and faces. Their clothes dropped to the ground in heaps. Nort and Crobbs watched, not thinking to move or speak until it was over and nine squirrels lay atop eight piles of guardsmen's uniforms and the drab clothing of the cook.

Frist was a reddish brown, and so was Monley. Lieutenant Staunton made a particularly striking squirrel, with a glorious gray pelt and tail. At first the squirrels simply lay there, and Nort wondered if his bespelled companions were even alive. But the little animals soon stirred, beginning to sit up, peer about, and scurry along the forest floor. One by one, the squirrels started to venture up the nearest tree trunks.

"Nort," Crobbs whispered, "do you suppose any of the other squirrels in this forest used to be guardsmen?"

Nort finally realized what he should have been doing

for the last minute or two. "I don't know. But we've got to catch them. How can we ever get them turned back if we don't?"

"They'll get mixed in with the other squirrels, elsewise," Crobbs said. "Can't say it'll be easy, though."

No, Nort thought. It wouldn't.

In a distant clearing, Dilly was the first to wake up. It took her a while to figure out what was wrong, and then she did a little scouting before she came back and poked Cam hard. "Cam, wake up!"

Cam rolled over in his blanket, prying his eyes open. "Dilly?"

"Meg's gone!"

Cam sat up. "She's not, um, attending to nature?"

Dilly shook her head, plopping down on her own blanket. "I checked. I couldn't find Lex, either. And their blankets are cold."

"So it's just us two left." Cam glanced over at Spinach. "Us three."

There was only one thing to do. "Let's pack up. We have to go look for them," Dilly said, practical as ever.

Cam grimaced. "I want to get out of this place. These trees"—he gestured to the great trunks and branches all around them—"aren't friendly. Not like my vegetable garden, is what I mean."

"I don't think enchanted forests like having people in them," Dilly said.

"Lex's carpet is still here," Cam pointed out, changing the subject. They both stared at the carpet, wondering if it would be willing to carry them.

As if in response to their stares, the carpet lifted itself up on one end. It stretched like a person just getting out of bed. Then it flopped into the air, where it swam lazily through the morning light, up and over the trees, and disappeared.

"It *was* here," Dilly said. And she leaned over to wake Spinach.

It is said that when you try to reach the edge of an enchanted forest, the forest amuses itself by leading you toward the center instead. Cam hoped this wasn't true. He and Dilly and Spinach were attempting to go south by traveling in a direction perpendicular to the path of the newly rising sun. They walked for a very long time before they found anything at all, and what they found was a stream. Since their water bags were nearly empty, this was a hopeful discovery, but no one moved to drink from the stream at first.

"Is this the same one?" Cam asked.

"It might be," Dilly said cautiously.

Spinach's success with the last stream had emboldened her. "I'm going to try," she announced, and she crouched down, reaching out to scoop up the water in her hands.

But behind them, someone hollered, *"Stop!"* Startled,

Spinach lost her balance and nearly fell into the stream. Instead Cam grabbed her arm and pulled her to her feet.

"Dilly?" Nort asked.

"Oh. It's you," Dilly said in a too-calm voice.

"Where's Meg?" Nort asked.

"She and Lex disappeared last night," Cam explained. "We were hoping we could find them."

Nort's companion, a big-boned young guardsman whose name Dilly didn't know, swung a leather bag off his shoulder. "Where should I put this?"

"Careful, Crobbs," Nort said wearily as the boy put the bag on the ground.

Dilly stepped closer to get a better look at Nort. "What happened to your face?"

Nort lifted one hand to his face and winced. "Squirrel bit me."

Now Dilly could see that Nort and Crobbs were scratched and bitten all over their arms and faces. "You got in a fight with a squirrel? Or a bunch of squirrels?"

"The other men drank from a stream, and they turned into squirrels," Nort said soberly. He gestured to the bag that Crobbs had set down. "We were only able to capture two of them." As they watched, the bag lurched sideways.

"Really? Because we drank from a stream, and nothing happened," Cam said.

"Then you were very lucky," said Nort. "Who's she?"

Dilly introduced Spinach, who immediately asked

Nort what it looked like when somebody turned into a
squirrel, and whether the squirrels seemed people-smart
or just squirrel-smart, and did he think that if the squirrels drank the water a second time, they would turn back
to people, or into something new, like beetles?

Nort looked alarmed by the onslaught, but he tried
to answer her questions. Dilly noticed that Crobbs carefully moved around the others so that he was as far away
from Spinach as possible. Cam just listened, smiling.
Nobody said anything more about the stream, but
nobody took a drink from it, either. Soon enough, the
little group of travelers began walking south, looking for
Meg and Lex, along with a way out of the enchanted
forest.

The scarf had been no help whatsoever in leading Meg
and Lex back to camp, and neither had a couple of finding spells Lex had cautiously tried. Those had resulted in
a series of darting red lights and a small storm, also the
unnerving sound of what seemed to be trees conversing
with each other in irritable tones. Lex and Meg had kept
still until it all died down, eventually taking shelter
under a non-talking tree to sleep for the rest of the
night. When morning came, neither of them felt very
hopeful about retracing their steps. "Let's just follow
your Laddy spell," Meg suggested. "It's been working this
whole time."

THE RUNAWAY DRAGON ✳ 111

"What about the others?" Lex asked, brushing off his black tunic as best he could.

"By now they'll be up and looking for us."

Lex thought this over. "So maybe they'll find us before we find them?"

"Maybe. At least we'll be going *somewhere*."

"Besides in circles, like last night."

"Exactly."

They hadn't gone far, though, before Meg told Lex, "My feet hurt."

"Mine, too," Lex said as they walked along in companionable misfortune. Meg was tempted to sit down and rest, but staying in one place, lost in the middle of this crazy forest, was unthinkable. So they trudged onward. The morning dragged like their feet. Meg managed to recall that when they had entered the enchanted forest yesterday, it had been a wonderful place. Today it wasn't.

"Don't you know any transportation spells?" Meg asked. "A little spell, one that wouldn't upset the forest?"

"I could try to call something." Lex didn't look very enthusiastic.

Meg stopped. "Why don't you?"

"Because you never know what might turn up."

Meg put her hands on her hips. At this point, she was willing to take a chance. "My feet *really, really* hurt!"

"All right, all right." Lex begrudgingly performed a

spell, not a very big one. Then he and Meg kept walking, unsure whether anything would happen.

The sun was high overhead when they heard a swishing noise and flinched. It was only Lex's magic carpet, accompanied by Meg's magic scarf. "Did your spell do this, or is it a coincidence?" Meg asked.

"Hard to tell." Lex eyed the rebellious rug. "I don't suppose you'd help us," he said. To Lex and Meg's surprise, the carpet slipped down toward them and hovered a few inches off the ground, as if inviting them along for a ride.

"Should we try it?" Lex asked Meg. His bones probably still ached from his last encounter with the magic carpet.

"Why not?" At the moment, Meg would have done anything to be able to travel without using her feet.

Meg and Lex climbed onto the carpet gingerly. "Dear most beauteous and magical Carpet," Lex said, attempting to sound sincere rather than distrustful, "please take us out of this forest."

"Southward," Meg put in.

"Southward."

"Your carpet *is* very pretty," Meg said, stroking the carpet's green-and-gold-and-rose back. The carpet arched a little beneath her touch as they lifted slowly into the air. Higher and higher they sailed, with Meg's scarf flying beside them like a lost piece of storm cloud. From

Meg's new vantage point, the forest resembled a deep green meadow.

The carpet was heading south. Lex let his breath out, still worried. If the carpet were to turn on them and tip them off at this height, their quest would end before they found Laddy *or* their lost friends. Lex spoke to Meg, trying to think of something else. "What is that up ahead?"

Meg squinted, shielding her eyes from the sun. "A really big tree?"

"It's moving," Lex said.

II

CAM AND THE OTHERS EMERGED FROM THE EN-
chanted forest into full sunlight and let out a
ragged cheer. A broad field of weeds and wild-
flowers spread out before them, flat at first before slop-
ing downward as if it were rushing to meet the hills they
could see in the distance. The three travelers tramped
across the field, feeling more hopeful than they had all
day. Dilly thought they should try to find the road again.
Cam said he figured it must be off to the left somewhere.
Then the earth shook, and everyone fell down. A moment later, the sun was gone and they were covered in
darkness.

"It's a giant!" Meg cried a heartbeat later.

"*A giant,*" Lex breathed. He and Meg stared, awestruck
by their first look at an actual giant. The towering trees
of the forest just reached the giant's chest. He was

dressed in a green shirt and brown trousers and he wore great leather boots, which made Meg wonder for an instant about giant cows. Except for its size, the giant's face looked like an ordinary man's. Of course, his red beard was the size and texture of a bramble hedge.

The giant crouched down, his face disappearing from sight. Only the vast arch of his back showed as he bent toward the ground. "What's he doing?" Meg asked. She wanted to fly away, but she couldn't bear to—not without knowing more about this immense and terrible person.

"Carpet," Lex said, "take us closer, but not too close."

The magic carpet must have been as curious as they were. It flew over the last stretch of forest and hovered next to the tree line, keeping to a respectable height.

Now they could see that the giant had dropped his hat on the ground, a hat as wide and round as the frog pond at home. At first Meg thought he'd done it by accident, but then she remembered seeing Cam trap a bird under his hat once. "I think he's caught something," she told Lex.

"That's a funny way of hunting," Lex said. "Maybe it's the white stag."

"Not outside the forest."

The giant slid one hand under the hat and flipped it over. Then he scrambled to pick up whatever he hadn't been able to flip into his hat.

Meg caught the smallest glimpse of what he was grabbing. "Lex!" she shrieked, practically diving off the carpet. "He has Dilly!" Meg banged Lex on the shoulder. "Do a spell! Stop him! Kill him! Do something, Lex!" Meg was shouting so loudly even the giant should be able to hear her.

The giant straightened, looking pleased with his catch.

Lex turned white. "We have to save them!"

"*You* have to save them!"

"Me?"

Meg nodded. "The wizard. My bodyguard. Remember? We have to help them. You have to help them."

Lex mimicked her nod. "All right. I could . . . I could . . . Maybe we can talk to him."

Meg knotted her hands into fists. "Lex," she hissed. "Can you or can't you conquer a giant with your magic?"

"I guess I could trip him," Lex said, troubled.

"*Trip* him?" Meg couldn't believe her ears. "How about slay him? He's a monstrous Dilly-stealer! He's probably taking her and Cam back to his castle to cook them for dinner! They'll be meatballs in his supper soup, and you won't even—"

"Meg," Lex said nervously. "Meg!"

Meg froze and looked over her shoulder. The giant's face was right beside them. "MORE THIEVES," the giant boomed in a voice so large it almost knocked Lex and Meg off the carpet.

"We're not thieves, we're wizards!" Lex shouted.

"WIZARDS?" the giant said. He didn't seem very impressed.

Meg leaned precariously over the edge of the carpet, trying to see into the giant's upturned hat, which rode in one of his huge hands, but the angle was all wrong.

With his other hand, the giant reached for the magic carpet, but it veered away. To Meg's astonishment, Lex convinced it to float up in front of the giant's face. "Wait!" Lex yelled. "Why are you taking those people in your hat?"

"I'M CATCHING HUMANS," the giant announced. "I'M GOING TO FIND THE ONE WHO STOLE MY GOLDEN FROBBLE." The giant reached for them again, but the carpet neatly avoided his grasp.

"Those people in your hat aren't thieves," Lex explained, still shouting. "They're our friends. They haven't stolen anything."

"MY DAUGHTER WILL LIKE THEM," the giant said, reluctantly lowering his hand. "I WILL KEEP CATCHING HUMANS TILL I FIND THE RIGHT ONE."

"What if we can find the thief for you?" Lex asked. "Will you give our friends back?"

Meg poked Lex. "Don't negotiate with him!" she ordered.

Lex ignored her, still talking to the giant. "Tell us what happened, and we'll bring the thief to you."

The giant looked thoughtful. "VERY WELL. MY NAME IS LORGLEY COMPROST, AND I AM OF THE SKY KINGDOM. A FORTNIGHT AGO, ONE OF YOUR KIND CAME KNOCKING ON MY DOOR. HE WAS PROPERLY RESPECTFUL, AND HE TOLD VERY GOOD JOKES. HE ATE MY BREAD AND SAT AT—WELL, ON—MY TABLE. MY WIFE AND I EVEN LET HIM SLEEP IN OUR HOME, IN MY DAUGHTER'S DOLLHOUSE. THE NEXT MORNING HE WAS GONE, WITHOUT THANKING US OR SAYING FAREWELL."

"What did he steal?" Meg yelled.

The giant continued. "TODAY WHEN I FINALLY UNLOCKED THE CUPBOARD WHERE I KEEP MY TREASURES, I SAW THAT THE GOLDEN FROBBLE WAS GONE. AND I KNEW THAT THE HORRIBLE LITTLE MAN MUST HAVE TAKEN IT."

"We'll find the horrible little man," Lex promised.

"AND THE FROBBLE," the giant prompted.

"And the frobble," Meg said. "What did the thief look like?"

"SMALL." Lorgley Comprost looked down into his hat. "I WILL TAKE GOOD CARE OF YOUR FRIENDS FOR FIVE DAYS. AFTER THAT . . ." He shrugged largely. "I WILL NO LONGER BELIEVE YOU MEANT WHAT YOU SAID."

"How many do you have in there?" Meg asked.

The giant counted swiftly. "FIVE."

"May we see them?" Lex asked.

The giant lifted the hat nearer to the magic carpet. Lex and Meg could see Dilly and Nort sprawled in the hat's crown. Spinach was sitting up rubbing her head, her braid tangled all around her, and Crobbs was crouched next to her clutching a leather bag—he seemed to be talking to it. As for Cam, he was climbing up the side of the hat. He was nearly to the top, too, but the giant flicked him with one massive finger, and he tumbled back down again.

"Cam!" Meg called.

Cam got to his feet. "Meg?"

"We've made a deal with the giant to help you," Lex cried. "We'll come back soon!"

Cam looked baffled and still stunned from his fall, but he managed to yell up at them, "Be careful!"

"We will!" Meg shouted back. Then she and Lex reluctantly settled themselves on the carpet again and watched the giant stride back up into the sky with their friends.

Meg could hardly bear to fly away, not knowing if Dilly was hurt, let alone leaving her and Cam and the others in the hands of a giant, but at least Lex had bought them a little time. Still. "Why couldn't you have done something to that giant and saved everybody?" she groused.

"Meg," Lex said pleadingly, looking younger than ever despite his bushy brows. "I don't like hurting people."

Meg wanted to say that the giant wasn't people, but she knew it wasn't true. Lorgley Comprost was a person, and he had been wronged by a human. It was just old-fashioned bad luck that had sent Meg's friends running right into an irate giant and his hat. "So you made a deal," Meg said.

"I made a deal." Lex folded his arms. "A promise, actually. Do you want them back or not?"

Meg was too frustrated to be sensible. "What about Laddy? You promised to help me find Laddy, too!"

"While we're looking for Laddy, we'll keep an eye out for villages," Lex said. "The thief had to come from somewhere. Besides, if I buy a few ingredients, I might be able to come up with a spell for tracking him down."

Meg gave him a look. "Like the ones you used to find our friends this morning?"

"It's different now that we're out of the forest," Lex said defensively.

Meg fell silent because she couldn't think of anything else to say. She and Lex flew southward without speaking. The world streamed by below them as they strained their eyes to catch a glimpse of a village, or better yet, a thief with a golden frobble slung over his shoulder.

"If we find Laddy, maybe he can help us with his dragon magic," Lex said at last.

"Dragon magic?"

"All dragons are magical. It'll show more when he's older, I suppose."

As Lex took out the shining scale to check their direction, Meg wondered how much magic a dragon usually learned from his mother and father. She felt a pang for Laddy, remembering the huge dragon bones in one corner of the cave where she had found him.

The carpet abruptly lifted higher to sail across another, smaller forest and a series of hills. Then it swooped over the top of the tallest hill and down the other side, and Meg was astonished by her first sight of the ocean, a vast expanse of shimmering blue-gray water. She was still staring at the amazing shine of it when Lex leaned forward, pointing. "Down there!"

Ahead of them, a village perched on the shore in a place where the land curved in as if the ocean had pushed harder there than anywhere else along the coast. Fishing boats lined the sand, with small houses jumbling up the hill above the dunes.

The carpet didn't show signs of slowing. Maybe it had its own destination and was just letting them tag along. "Carpet," Meg said, "wouldn't you like to rest in that lovely seaside village?"

Lex pointed to one side. "Or in that evil fortress?"

"How do you know it's evil?" Meg asked, but even as the words came out of her mouth, she saw what Lex was talking about. The fortress on the mountainside loomed darkly over the small village, all shadow-colored stones and harsh bulwarks and closed iron gates. "Oh." It did look sort of evil.

Lex checked Laddy's scale. "This is where Laddy landed next," Lex said.

Meg reminded herself that her dragon might not be in this place anymore. But they had found the next step in Laddy's journey.

The scarf drifted downward, the magic carpet tilting to follow it. They landed in the village, not at the fortress, but Meg and Lex weren't about to argue with that. Though neither of them said so, they weren't in a hurry to meet whoever lived in the stone monstrosity on the hill. "Maybe Laddy's here in the village," Meg said too brightly as she and Lex walked along the village's only street.

"Maybe," Lex said. "I'm hungry."

"We'll have to find someone to sell us food." They'd left their packs and food at the lost campsite, but Meg had a few coins in her pocket. Cam had given them to her. "Just in case," he'd said, and now "in case" had happened.

It seemed they might have trouble finding anyone to ask about food, however. The village was far too quiet. The only sound Meg could hear was the distant mumble of the surf. All of the windows were shuttered and all of the doors were closed. Lex tried knocking on a few, and

Meg called out, but there was no answer. "Where is everybody?" The village didn't seem old enough to be abandoned. The houses were made of plaster painted in yellows and blues and oranges and greens, and the paint hadn't faded or peeled. The flowers in the window boxes were dead, though. Cam would have known how long it had been since they'd been watered just by looking. "I don't think Laddy's in the village," Meg added disconsolately.

Lex gazed at the scale as if he could read it, then turned to face the fortress. "No. He went up there."

"Of course." Where else would Laddy have gone? Meg started trying door handles.

"What are you doing?" Lex asked her. "Aren't we going to the fortress?"

"First we're finding some food. Since nobody's using it, anyway."

"Right." Lex checked the other side of the street. A few doors later, they found one that wasn't locked and went inside. Meg remembered the witch's house and hoped there wouldn't be any more bodies. Lex must have been thinking the same thing because he said, "Maybe they're all dead of a mysterious plague and we'll—"

Meg elbowed him. "Don't say that."

The room they stepped into was a kitchen with a table and four chairs. Cooking pots hung from hooks on the wall above a tidy metal stove. A green vase holding the remains of a bouquet of daisies decorated the center of the table forlornly. To Meg's relief, the only thing lying on the bed in the back room was a faded green-and-yellow striped quilt.

Lex poked around in the little kitchen. He discovered some biscuits in a wooden box, which was probably why they hadn't been eaten by mice. Meg scrounged up a bucket, which led to a hunt for the village well. The water was cool and clear. "Not enchanted," Lex said with satisfaction.

12

MEG AND LEX TOOK THEIR BISCUITS AND WELL water down to the shore to eat so that Meg could see the ocean up close. As they walked across the sand, Meg marveled at the way it gave beneath her feet.

"Take your boots off," Lex told her, and Meg did. She loved that the long-legged birds ran nimbly along next to the water, where the sand was damp and gave beneath her feet in a different way. She managed to touch the ocean itself without getting entirely wet, though it was a near thing and made Lex laugh. Meg licked her finger, pleased to find the water was salty, a thing she had privately doubted when she'd heard it from her tutors. She and Lex sat down on the dry sand just out of reach of the waves to eat their biscuits.

Meg's capricious scarf and Lex's cantankerous rug showed up again during the impromptu picnic. The cloth creatures flew low over the waves, trying to shove each other into the water. Lex frowned. "If my carpet gets waterlogged, it won't be able to stay up." The carpet must have figured this out on its own because, not long after Lex had spoken, it went up the beach and lay there, apparently sunbathing. The scarf, which hadn't gotten as wet, settled for scaring stray seagulls, sneaking up behind them and pulling their tail feathers.

Meg wanted to stay here forever, watching the slide and spill of waves striking the shore. Instead she finished off her last biscuit and gave Lex a dark look.

"The fortress?" he asked.

"The fortress," Meg said. Lex began brushing the sand off his feet to put his boots back on, and Meg did the same. Reluctantly, she turned her back on the ocean, following Lex up the incline to the village. They put the bucket where it belonged in the house where they'd found the biscuits, and left one of Meg's coins on the table. Then Meg and Lex walked up the hill toward the fortress.

Riding in a giant's hat wasn't something Dilly ever cared to do again. She had come awake only to find that her head hurt and she was being bounced along inside a great rough bowl. Or that's what it felt like. Nort soon explained where she really was. *"What?"* Dilly said.

"A giant. See?"

Dilly looked up. Something red and bushy tilted and waved high above her.

"That's his beard," Nort explained.

Dilly braced herself on the floor of the upturned hat. "We're up in the sky?" she said, hoping he would tell her something different this time.

"Oh," Nort said, remembering, "you're afraid of heights, aren't you?"

Dilly closed her eyes. "A little, maybe." She made herself open her eyes and look around. Cam sat patiently untangling Spinach's braid, no easy task when every few seconds they were jolted and thumped from side to side. Crobbs was holding his pack tightly, careful to keep the two enchanted squirrels from escaping. And then there was Nort. "When you didn't come back from chasing the stag, we figured you were dead in a demon pit," she told him between jounces.

He eyed her. "Would you have minded?"

Dilly mulled this over. "Some."

Her answer seemed to satisfy Nort, though an instant later they forgot all about it when the hat lurched mightily. Dilly tried very hard not to think about how high up they must be. Being in the bottom of a hat didn't feel high; it felt low. Or so she told herself, and kept telling herself.

After a long while and many more scrapes and bruises, the hat came to a stop. If any of them had been able to see out instead of up, they would have known that it was sitting on Lorgley Comprost's kitchen table. A fact that did not please Lorgley's wife in the least.

"HANG YOUR HAT UP," she told him. "DON'T GO PUTTING IT ON MY CLEAN TABLE!"

"THERE'S SOMETHING IN IT," he explained. "LITTLE CREATURES LIKE THE THIEF."

"YOU BROUGHT HOME *MORE*?" she said, outraged.

"NOW, KITTY. I WENT TO THE BELOWLANDS LOOKING FOR THE THIEF AND CAPTURED THESE HUMANS. THEIR FRIENDS, WHO ARE WIZARDS, HAVE PROMISED TO FIND THE THIEF FOR ME."

"HMPH." Kitty Comprost peered into the hat, offering its denizens a view up her giant nostrils. "WHAT ARE YOU GOING TO DO WITH THEM IN THE MEANTIME? BESIDES GETTING THEM OFF MY TABLE?" She swept up the hat and stood before her husband, waiting for the right answer.

"I THOUGHT LORIS COULD PLAY WITH THEM."

"OH." The giant's wife smiled at last. "THAT'S SO THOUGHTFUL!" She bellowed for her daughter, and everyone in the hat covered their ears. "LORIS! COME HERE!"

Loris thundered into the kitchen. "WHAT, MOMMY?" Loris was five years old and very fond of dollies.

Her hair was yellow, like her mother's, and stuck out in pigtails on either side of her head.

"DADDY BROUGHT YOU SOME LITTLE PEO-PLE TO PLAY WITH."

Loris's father cleared his throat. "BUT BE CARE-FUL WITH THEM. I HAVE TO GIVE THEM BACK IN FIVE DAYS."

Kitty raised her brows.

"IF THE WIZARDS BRING ME MY THIEF," he said.

She nodded and spoke to Loris. "YOU HEARD YOUR FATHER. PLAY NICELY WITH THE HU-MANS. DADDY'S TAKING THEM BACK SOON."

Loris had grabbed the edge of the hat her mother was holding and was looking into it. She didn't seem to be listening.

"DO YOU HEAR ME, LORIS?" her mother asked.

Still looking into the hat, Loris recited, "YES-I-HAVE-TO-BE-CAREFUL-WITH-THEM-BECAUSE-DADDY-HAS-TO-TAKE-THEM-BACK."

"GOOD GIRL," Lorgley said.

"OH," Loris cried, enchanted. "ONE OF THEM HAS LONG, LONG HAIR!"

"Are we just going to knock on the door?" Lex asked.

"Yes." They were almost to the fortress.

"Don't you think the owners are evil?"

"Yes. But they have Laddy."

Lex stopped. "Meg, we should have a rescue plan."

Meg stopped, too. "I have a rescue plan. The first part of the plan is to find out what's going on."

"By just asking? Shouldn't we sneak in and spy around?"

"How? Do you have a spell?"

"I have a lot of spells," Lex said.

"Then we'll be fine," Meg told him, hoping she was right.

Five minutes later, Meg and Lex were being surrounded by the fortress's evil guards, who were dressed in black armor, naturally. Meg didn't think there was really a metal like that. Maybe they had painted it? Or maybe it was magic. The guards had long legs. Meg had to trot a little to keep up. "Could you please slow down?" she asked breathlessly. But the guard holding her arm didn't speak. He merely rushed her across the bridge and shoved her through the great iron gates of the fortress.

Meg glanced over at her fellow prisoner. Lex shrugged, which Meg took to mean he was saving his magic till they were inside and found out what was going on. It didn't seem very useful to argue with twenty evil guards in black armor. As soon as Meg and Lex learned if Laddy was there, they could make a clever new plan. Or so Meg told herself, although being in this place made her uneasy, just as it was intended to do.

Loris Comprost had a simply beautiful dollhouse. It was half as tall as she was and sat on its very own table in her bedroom. It was painted pink with white shutters. For the insides, her father had carved little chairs and tables and cupboards, while her mother had made miniature curtains for the windows, upholstery for the sofas, and rugs for the floors. Loris pulled her old doll family out of the dollhouse, her love for them dying abruptly in the excitement of the new arrivals.

Loris was an expert on dollies, but she'd never had dolls that walked and talked before, let alone ones that got hungry. The new dollies discovered that Loris was quite reasonable when it came to certain things, like getting bread crumbs from the kitchen for her dollies' tea parties. She was less understanding about bath-room needs, and she was toweringly unreasonable about grooming and other matters. She insisted on putting Crobbs to bed in an upstairs room filled with oversized furniture which probably appeared perfectly refined to giant eyes, but which was full of splinters and knots from a human perspective. The blanket alone was heavy enough to smother a person. It was more like a coarsely woven tent.

Crobbs was thinking about getting out of bed, but then Loris threatened in motherly tones to squash him if he didn't stay there. He stayed—even when she managed to pry open the pack with a pin and let the squirrels out.

The squirrels were on the floor in a flash, moving so

fast that Loris hardly noticed them. Nort saw them racing down the stairs and ran to catch them, but they hur-
tled between his legs and along the front hall before
disappearing out the dollhouse door.

"Goodbye, Lieutenant Staunton," Nort said softly.

Loris had already lost interest in the pack. She made
Cam sit in a flowered armchair in the parlor. He stood
up and she pushed him back down with one giant finger,
nearly breaking his ribs. Cam sat there miserably while
Loris retrieved Nort, snatching him up from the sadly
squirrel-free stairway and dropping him onto a sofa-like
object beside Cam's chair. Next Loris got down to the
serious business of Dilly's and Spinach's hair.

Dilly's hair didn't get very much attention, though.
Loris plied a huge-toothed comb on Dilly's dark locks, but
not for long. Loris soon turned to her favorite new dolly,
Spinach. "MOMMY'S GOING TO CO-O-O-MB YOUR
HAIR, AND MOMMY'S GOING TO WA-A-A-SH
YOUR HAIR." Loris laid Spinach's hair out in a long,
long line. "AND MOMMY'S GOING TO CU-U-U-T
YOUR HAIR, TOO." Loris twirled Spinach's hair around
her fingers as Spinach turned a stricken look on Dilly.

"Just be glad we're still alive," Dilly told Spinach.

"Is she really going to cut my hair?" Spinach whispered.

"I'M GOING TO CALL YOU ROSALINA LILI-
ANA," Loris announced to Spinach. The giant child

poked Dilly, obviously less impressed. "YOU CAN BE THE FRIEND DOLL. COOKIE ANN."

"Rosalina Liliana," Dilly said to Spinach snidely, feeling a little miffed at her second-rate status.

"Cookie Ann," Spinach replied through gritted teeth.

Dilly tried talking to Loris, but Loris kept saying "WHAT?" and quickly lost interest in actual conversation with her new toys. She seemed to prefer pretend conversation. "IS THE FRIEND DOLL SAYING FRIENDLY THINGS? COOKIE ANN WANTS MORE TEA AND CRUMBS, DOESN'T SHE, ROSALINA LILIANA?"

"Yes," Spinach said. "More crumbs." Anything was better than having her hair combed by Loris.

But Loris, when she went, must have forgotten about the crumbs. Instead she came back carrying the biggest pair of scissors Dilly and Spinach had ever seen.

The fortress guards marched Meg and Lex up a long flight of stone stairs into a huge throne room that looked like what Lex's drawing room had always wanted to be when it grew up. The place was decorated entirely in dire metal and stone. Its floor was black marble, and it was lined with heavy matching columns that appeared to be chained into place—with chains whose links were each as long as Meg's arm. More of the armor-clad warriors lined the walls on either side. A dozen ravens flew over-head, scribing ominous patterns in the air and causing Meg to wince at the thought that they might drop some-thing on her head.

At the end of the vast hall, someone was seated on an elaborate black-and-gold throne. The ruler of the fortress awaited their coming with evident disdain. After what seemed like an eternity of walking, Meg and Lex reached the throne, or were allowed to approach within ten feet of it. At that point, the nearest guard shoved Meg to her knees. "Bow before Her Supremacy the Empress of the Southern Reaches." Lex got shoved, too, Meg noticed.

The figure on the throne stood up and stretched. "You can call me Malison."

To Meg's surprise, the ruler was a girl about her own age. Maybe she was even a year or two younger. Malison wore a slithery black dress. Her black hair was piled up on her head in snaky curls. Her skin was very pale, and her lips were very red. Black patterns swirled down her bare arms clear to her red-nailed fingertips.

"You're just a girl!" Meg blurted.

"Just a girl?" Malison sneered. "*I* am a sorceress, the greatest magic-maker the world has ever known."

Meg waited for Lex to challenge the girl, to tell Mal-ison that he was a *far* greater magic-maker than she was. But he said nothing. Meg looked over at her friend, only to find him staring at the sorceress with open envy. With envy, and with something more. Meg looked at Malison again, trying to see what Lex was seeing. Finally it came to her. When Lex wore black, he looked like he was playing dress-up. But on Malison, black was just perfect.

13

"YOU'RE AN EVIL SORCERESS, AREN'T YOU?" SAID Meg.

"How clever of you to guess. What are you, a princess on a quest or something?"

When Meg didn't answer, Malison started to laugh. "You *are*? How dismal of you!"

"What's wrong with quests?" Meg asked.

"*Everything* is wrong with quests. They're so goody-goody," Malison said, waving one hand dismissively. "Wait—is your quest to defeat me? Is that why you're here?" She seemed a little too enthusiastic for Meg's current mood. "You could try really hard, and then fail miserably, and then languish in my dungeons for . . ." The sorceress made a show of thinking deeply, then continued, "Oh, forever."

Meg decided that she didn't like this Malison person, and that she'd better not ask about Laddy. She probably wouldn't like the answer. "Do some magic," Meg said to Lex under her breath, but he didn't appear to be listening.

Malison smiled, shaking her head. "Did you just tell him to do some magic? Is he a wizard or something?"

Lex started. "I *am* a wizard, Empress. At your service." Lex bowed awkwardly.

"Lex!" Meg said, but he wasn't listening.

Lex took a step or two closer to Malison. "I know we just met, but I think your fortress, and your guards, and your hair, and your fingernails are wonderful, and maybe we could talk about magic together?"

Malison shot a triumphant look at Meg before she said in fake-nice tones, "Why, what a good idea. We'll do that a little later."

"If you aren't going to do any magic, then I will," Meg told Lex, not bothering to keep her voice down, since Malison apparently had the hearing of a bat, and for his part, Lex had gone deaf.

But this got his attention. "Now, Meg," he said, alarmed, "that's not necessary. I'll, I could . . ." But then Lex looked at Malison and lost his focus. "Isn't she *beautiful*?" he whispered.

"She's gorgeous," Meg said soothingly. To Malison she said, "What did you do, put a spell on him?"

Malison laughed again. Meg suspected she had practiced that laugh, which managed to be both tinkly and menacing at the same time. "I simply have this effect on men." She waved her hand at the guards. "It comes with the territory."

"The evil-sorceress territory."

"Of course," Malison said smugly.

Meg began muttering a spell—muttering because that was how spells were always said, not because she thought Malison wouldn't be able to hear her. Well, all right, Meg was a little worried that she'd mispronounce a word and Malison would laugh at her yet again. As it was, the Empress of the Southern Reaches didn't seem at all concerned. Meg tried not to think about what that meant. The spell she'd chosen was supposed to cause a magic mist, which she thought might allow her to grab Lex by the wrist and get out of the throne room.

Meg finished the spell and tried to stand proud, a princess of Greeve in all her glory. Or in all her good intentions, anyway. Just because none of her spells had turned out right *yet* didn't mean they never would.

As usual, something did happen. Behind her, Meg could hear several soft thudding noises. In front of her, Malison frowned, which Meg thought was a good sign. "What have you done?" the young sorceress demanded. She sounded more annoyed than anything else.

Meg turned to look. At first she couldn't even tell what had happened. Then Malison said incredulously, "You turned my ravens into *waffles*?"

Sure enough, there were a dozen pale brown squares dotting the black marble floor of the great hall. Not a single raven remained—at least not in its former shape.

"Yes, waffles," Meg said bravely, facing Malison. "Who knows what I'll do next?" Which was quite true.

"*I* know," Malison said, still annoyed. "You'll sit in one of my dungeons while I decide what to do with you."

"You can't just lock us up," Meg began, but Malison interrupted her.

"Us? No. Just you. Lex and I are going to have a nice talk and drink some tea."

Lex's glazed expression vanished. "Tea? She means hot chocolate, doesn't she, Meg?"

"Hot chocolate it is," Malison said quickly, and Lex relaxed into a hopeful daze. Malison raised her voice. "Where's my chief guard?"

Meg thought of Hanak, her father's guard captain, with an odd burst of homesickness. But Malison's chief guard, when he appeared, wasn't anything like Hanak. In fact, he looked an awful lot like—"Bain?" Meg blurted.

Bain turned unfriendly eyes on Meg. "Do I know you, miss?" he asked.

But Malison answered before Meg could. "Don't listen to anything the prisoner says. Just take her to the dungeons."

"Yes, mistress," Bain said, and there was warmth in his voice now that he was talking to Malison. But there wasn't laughter. It shocked Meg to see his familiar face so serious, all of the deviltry gone from his eyes. He was older now, which also surprised her. Of course he was dressed in black armor. Even his black curls were slicked back in a severe, but arguably eviler, style. Meg's heart sank. How had he come to be a dread sorceress's guard?

Meg tried to keep her dismay from showing. "They *are* under a spell," Meg told the girl. "That's cheating."

"Whatever. Take her away," Malison said.

"Yes, mistress," Bain said again, stepping forward.

"Wait," Malison said. "I'll admit I'm curious. How do you know my chief guard's name?"

Meg lifted her head. "I'm not telling."

Malison laughed, and this time her laugh wasn't tinkly at all. "You'll tell. When your flesh is rotting off your bones—or perhaps slightly before that—you'll tell."

"Lex!" Meg called. "Do something!"

But Lex didn't seem to hear her. Instead he looked around, confused, as if trying to identify the source of the sound, even as Meg was escorted away by Bain and two other guards.

Meg did try to talk to Bain as she walked down a series of long dark halls and stone stairways, deep into the bowels of the fortress. But he wouldn't listen. He was clearly following orders. Meg kept pestering him even though she could tell it was useless. She reminded the former bandit of the adventures they'd been through a year ago. His stoic demeanor only cracked once, when Meg said, "And then you threw a sword to Alya, don't you remember?"

"Alya," Bain said in a slightly different tone. He shook his head and gave Meg a little shove forward. "Alya is a traitor."

"Traitor to who?" Meg asked, shocked.

"Why, to the empress," another guard told her, as if it were obvious.

After that Meg really was silent until she reached her cell and was put inside. For an instant she dared to hope that Bain was faking, that he'd wink at her as he turned the heavy key in the lock and then come back later to let her out. That it was all part of another one of his elaborate schemes. But he didn't even look at her as he locked the door and marched away with his two men.

"Well," Meg said, sitting down on the narrow cot. "That wasn't nearly as much fun as I thought it would be." She wasn't sure if she meant confronting the owner of the fortress or seeing Bain again, but it didn't much matter, anyway.

Night fell over the dollhouse—or seemed to fall. It wasn't actually night yet, but Loris had said that it was nap time and had thrown a blanket over the top of the dollhouse so her new toys would go to sleep while she went off to have her dinner. The blanket was very effective, and it took a little time, along with a new collection of bruises, before the captives could gather in the living room to talk.

"She's a deadly foe," Nort said. Everyone knew who he meant.

"She doesn't mean to be unkind," Spinach ventured. "She's *cute*."

They tried to picture the giant Loris as cute. It wasn't easy.

"She cut your hair," Dilly reminded Spinach.

Spinach's face fell, and she tugged at her hair, distracted. Spinach without her hair was a strange sight. Her pale locks hung lankly around her face, barely touching her shoulders. She hadn't asked them any questions since her hair had been cut, which wasn't like her in the least.

"Loris is a child," Cam said. "It's just our misfortune she's so large, and our prison-keeper, too."

"Misfortune?" Nort snorted in the darkness. "I don't know which is worse, the squirrels or this."

"Don't forget that Meg and Lex are going to come back and help us," Cam said.

"By doing what?" Dilly asked, but no one had an answer.

"We have to escape. It's the only way," Nort said.

They were all in agreement with him. The only question was how.

When Loris reappeared, she was not happy to see that her new dolls were in the living room. "*NO*, ROSALINA LILIANA. *NO*, COOKIE ANN. YOU SHOULD BE IN THE KITCHEN. YOU MUST STAY WHERE I PUT YOU."

Then it occurred to Loris that she had brought food. "But since it is time for your supper, I will let you be in the kitchen for a little while." There wasn't really enough room around the table for five people, but Loris shoved and the five of them managed to fit into the kitchen, if not exactly at the table. They were very hungry by now, and Loris was pleased to see them eat their crumbs and bits of meatball with such enthusiasm.

After supper, Loris put her small prisoners back where she said they belonged, though she mixed up Crobbs and Nort, putting Nort to bed and Crobbs in the living room with Cam. They tried not to fuss as she jammed them into their respective spots. Being lifted in giant fingers that were far more careless than they intended to be was painful, Nort thought, especially when a body was already bruised from being banged back and forth inside a giant hat.

It was easier to be patient with Loris now that they had a plan for escaping from her clutches, of course. They were waiting for the moment when Loris and her parents would go to bed. Dilly thought maybe Loris would try to put every single one of her "dolls" to bed, too, but the giant child lost track of her attempts to make the captives' activities match her own once supper was over. The five of them stayed where she had put them earlier, listening as Loris went up the hall to the bathroom. They could hear faint sounds of water splashing and of Loris complaining. Cam was certain face washing was involved. He felt a flash of sympathy, recalling how he had avoided having his own face scrubbed when he was a little boy.

A few minutes later, Loris's mother returned with her daughter to tuck her in, and Loris showed her mommy what she'd done with the prisoners. They stayed very still, hoping Kitty Comprost wouldn't think to lock them up in some way for the night. The giant woman had her doubts. She asked her daughter, "DO YOU THINK YOUR LITTLE TOYS WILL BE ALL RIGHT?"

Loris was more confident than her mother. "YES, MOMMY. THEY HAD THEIR DINNER AND THEY'RE GOING TO BED NOW. JUST LIKE ME."

"To bed" sitting at the kitchen table, Dilly thought, looking across the rough table at Spinach with a wry expression. Spinach smiled back.

Kitty Comprost's face must have seemed doubtful still because Loris said, "I COULD PUT THE BLAN-KET BACK." With a heavy rustling sound, darkness fell over the dollhouse again. Darkness, and a stuffiness to the air.

"THAT'S BETTER," Loris's mother said. "NOW WINK-BINK INTO BED YOU GO."

"GOOD NIGHT, MOMMY."

"GOOD NIGHT, LITTLE ONE."

Dilly smothered her laugh. Compared to Kitty Comprost, Loris really was little.

Even after the candles were blown out and the darkness deepened with Kitty's departure, none of them dared to move for a long while, fearful that the giant child would hear them and get up to see what they were doing. But they could easily hear her breathing, and they waited as agreed till her breathing grew slow and even, telling them that Loris had fallen asleep. Then the five prisoners gathered in the dollhouse living room once more.

14

I T DIDN'T TAKE LONG FOR MEG TO CONCLUDE that being a prisoner was boring. At least when she had been riding through the enchanted forest, there were things to look at. But she quickly ran out of things to look at in her cell. About the only interesting item in it was a spider, and the spider mostly sat on its web in a high corner, waiting motionlessly for a fly that didn't seem to know it was supposed to make an appearance.

Malison's laughter was still ringing in her ears, but even so, Meg attempted to use the only weapon she had at her disposal: her mixed-up magic. She managed to tint one of the walls of her cell a very pale shade of blue, change the iron bars on the door to an even stronger metal she'd never seen before, and make her blanket disappear before she gave up in disgust.

Hours later, someone brought Meg a tray of food.

She caught a glimpse of the old woman's face peering in at her through the small barred window at the top of the door before the tray slid through a slot at the bottom. Meg sprang to her feet. "Wait!" she said. "Are you enchanted, too?"

The woman glanced over her shoulder. "Do I look like a man?"

"No," Meg said, though truth be told, the woman had a bit of a mustache. In fact, Meg thought maybe she'd seen that particular mustache before. "Aren't you one of Alya's people?" Meg asked.

"Maybe. Who are you?"

"I'm Meg." Meg realized the name might not mean much. "Princess Margaret of Greeve?"

"*That* one." The old woman nearly left.

"Please—what's your name?"

"Stefka." Named, the woman seemed more inclined to linger for a moment.

"Can you tell me what's going on? Where's Alya?"

"She's locked up down the way," Stefka explained. "Alya wouldn't wait on the grand mistress. Went after that empress like a pack of wolves before they stopped her," the woman said proudly.

"How did this whole thing happen?"

"We were tending to our own business, making a life for ourselves down in the village, when this fortress appeared on the hill. Overnight it was."

"That's not good," Meg said.

"No. The next day, the girl-who-calls-herself-empress popped up in the middle of the village and ordered us to gather together Alya's people, the fisher-folk, farmers from up the valley, everyone."

"Couldn't you have run away?"

Stefka shook her head. "She called us with magic and we came, like it or not."

"Oh," Meg said, understanding.

"Inside of an hour, she had stolen Alya's gold and made us her servants. But the men . . ." Stefka's face was a study. "She has a spell laid on them, makes them think she's really an empress. Alya's brother is the worst one, chief-guarding about the fortress like he was born to it. The rest of us are no more than slaves, cooking her fancy meals and washing her black gowns and polishing her black marble floors."

Meg wondered if Malison's food was black, too, but she had more important questions to ask. "So none of the women are under a spell?"

"Unless being locked up is a spell," Stefka grumbled. "After those fool boys in black armor threw Alya in the dungeon, the rest of us shut our mouths and started scrubbing." She looked over her shoulder again. "I'd best be going."

"I don't suppose you could let me out? You could say it was a mistake."

"Don't have the key," the old woman said reasonably. "Eat up, Princess." Then she was gone.

Meg was still bored, but she had a thing or two to think about now—such as how the stag spell and now Malison's spell only affected men. She tried to imagine a spell that would only affect women, but all she could picture was how silly her mother's ladies-in-waiting acted. Meg shook her head. At least she had supper—though the food should have been bread and water, if she knew anything about dungeons. Apparently Malison had forgotten to specify that the prisoners be given nasty food. Of course, anything would taste good to someone who'd only had stale biscuits to eat lately. Meg bit into her turnips and chicken with gusto.

Nort and his four fellow prisoners took down the curtains in the dollhouse and tied them together to make a rope. It wasn't easy to make the rope in the darkness, but they managed to work together with only one mishap, when Crobbs fell down the stairs. Nort winced in sympathy, thinking that Crobbs could ill afford another bump on the head.

At last the rope was finished. The others passed sections of the rope to Cam, who secured it on a rafter and fed it out the window.

"Do you really think it's long enough?" Spinach asked. She must have been feeling a little better, because she followed this up with, "Have you ever climbed down a rope before?" and "Do you want to use my hair instead?"

"Your hair's gone, Spinach," Dilly pointed out. Although it had seemed longer at dinner, now that she thought about it. "Is it growing back already?"

Spinach touched her hair. It had been shoulder length this evening, but now it reached to the middle of her back. "Oh. A little."

"Besides, the curtain-rope will work." Dilly hoped she sounded calm. She wasn't thinking about how high up they were, not at all. Not her.

As they got ready to climb down the rope, Dilly moved away from the window, bumping Nort with her shoulder as she went. "Do you want me to help you?" he asked. "She's afraid of being up so high," he explained to the others.

"Well, sort of," Dilly mumbled, humiliated. Nort privately figured it was worth having her mad at him if she got the help that she needed.

"Maybe Crobbs can bring her down," Cam said.

"I'll do it," Nort said.

"Crobbs is bigger," Spinach said. "He should do it."

Nort didn't say anything else, though he automatically tried to stand a little taller. He was still shorter than Cam and Crobbs—he knew that even in the dark. The important thing was getting Dilly down, he told himself. "I'll go first, to check that it's safe," Nort said, trying to reinforce his image.

No one argued, so Nort climbed out the window. The rope swayed and swung about in the slim shaft of moonlight that shone through Loris's bedroom window as he descended. He continued to the very end of the curtain-rope before he looked down. To his dismay, the rope didn't reach the floor beneath him. He guessed he must be about five feet off the floor by human standards. Nort wondered how giants would have measured it even as he made himself let go.

He hit the ground hard and rolled. As he lay there catching his breath, he could hear questioning voices from above. "I'm fine," he called, pretty sure his own tiny voice wouldn't disturb Loris. "It's close, and I'll help you." But how? Nort bumbled around in the dim light as Cam began to descend, and then he saw it: Loris had left one of her socks on the floor, half-hidden under the dollhouse table or her mother would have surely made her pick it up.

The sock was heavier than he thought it would be. Nort slid it across the wooden floor till it was lying beneath the dangling rope. He got it in position just before Cam dropped to the floor. Cam's landing was much softer than Nort's had been, and Nort smiled with satisfaction at his own ingenuity.

One by one the others climbed down the rope. Or two by two, in Dilly's case. She had gotten very quiet and had edged away into the dollhouse, but Spinach brought her back. Crobbs put one muscular arm around her, talking in the same tones he'd used to soothe the squirrels as he came down the rope with Dilly in tow.

Speaking of squirrels, Nort heard a small sound and glanced up to see the two escapees skittering down the rope. "Lieutenant?" he said, but the squirrels leaped off the rope and disappeared into the darkness.

"Come on," Nort told the others. "We'd better be gone before sunrise."

It wasn't easy to sleep on a cot in a dungeon, especially without a blanket. Meg dozed on and off. The torch on the wall outside her door cast a square of barred light across the rough floor. Very late that night, Meg woke up and looked sleepily at the patch of light, only to realize that something was different. She sat up. A black line was painting itself across the floor, crossing the shadows of the bars. Meg got up and crouched for a closer look. Then she laughed. A line of ants was trailing its way toward her abandoned dinner plate.

Meg thought almost fondly of Quorlock. "So, are you here to help me?" she asked the ants, not expecting an answer.

But the line paused and blurred a bit. The ants broke rank and painstakingly re-formed. To Meg's amazement, they appeared to be spelling out letters. And what they spelled out was "no."

"No? But I helped you. Or—your cousins. I went around an anthill in the forest."

This time it took longer for the ants to spell their

reply: "common courtesy." They seemed to confer a little afterward, however. Then they spelled out, a bit begrudgingly, "thanks."

That was all Meg could get out of them. They were obviously too busy with food transportation and distribution to bother any further with a human girl. Of course, if what Quorlock had said was true, the only thing the ants could have done for her was sort grain, and Meg didn't have any barley mixed with millet. She lay back down to watch the ants at their work until she fell asleep again.

Meg woke for the second time because of a sound. Listening herself awake, she knew that something was creeping across the floor. Meg pretended to shift in her sleep so she could turn and open her eyes a crack to see what it was. By this time the torch was burning low. A dungeon cell in darkness would be far worse, especially with things crawling around inside. Meg shuddered and strained her eyes the more, trying to identify her intruder.

The shadowy creature was bigger than an ant, but it was smaller than Meg's fist. It not only scratched, it occasionally clinked as it made its way slowly across the floor toward her. Meg stopped pretending to be asleep and sat up. The thing could have been a mouse, although it was oddly shaped. "Hello?" Meg said.

The mouse froze, but it didn't run away. After a

moment, Meg realized that it was waiting for her to do something. She slipped off her cot and sank down to the floor. "What is it?"

The mouse wasn't shaped wrong, she concluded; it was carrying something, and the object was too large for it to carry comfortably. Instead the mouse had dragged whatever-it-was across the floor. The mouse tried to raise the object, but it wasn't strong enough, and the weight fell back down with a little *clink*. Meg put out her hand to touch the thing. Metal. She took it from the mouse as gently as possible and felt as much as saw that it was an iron key.

"I saved a mouse from a hawk," Meg said, remembering. Free from the weight of the key, the mouse gave her a little bow.

"Thank you very much," Meg said. She wanted to say, "You're nicer than the ants," but who knew—maybe the ants had called the mouse. It's not like the ants could have brought the key to her. So instead she resorted to court diplomacy language, proclaiming, "You are a true friend and have well repaid a debt of honor this night."

The mouse bowed one last time before it scurried across the floor, squeezed beneath the door, and disappeared.

Meg smiled, holding the key in her hands. Good old Quorlock! He might talk too much, and he didn't understand about girls in towers, but he knew a thing or two about enchanted forests, not to mention quests.

15

UCKILY, THE GIANT CHILD'S MOTHER HAD LEFT the bedroom door open. Small though they were, Cam knew they wouldn't have fit through the crack beneath the door. As it was, the five of them were able to leave Loris's room and walk silently down the hallway. In the near darkness, it was like traveling along a canyon, with the ceiling as high as a sky overhead. They hadn't gone far when Nort tripped over the head of one of the nails holding the floorboards down. Then Dilly gashed her leg on a dagger-sized splinter and they had to stop to bind up the wound with a handkerchief.

Cam ranged a little ahead while Spinach ministered to Dilly's leg. He nearly fell down himself when he ran into something thigh-high, but it gave a little, and Cam realized it must be a rug. He climbed up to walk along it and promptly got his foot stuck down between two bunches of cloth. It was a rag rug, apparently. Cam wrestled with the rug, trying to free his foot. Finally he was able to get loose and rejoin the group. "There's a rug up ahead," he said nonchalantly. "It's pretty hard to walk on."

"We should keep to the side of the hall," Dilly said.

As they crept along the wall, well away from the treacherous rug, Cam thought he knew why mice usually stayed to the edges of a room. He was glad that in the Belowlands, at least, he wasn't really a mouse. Cam felt a pang of homesickness for his nice quiet life in Greeve. He missed his garden, the peaceful green of his squash vines and the hopeful two-leafed look of seedlings when they first sprouted.

It was a long journey to the kitchen.

When they got there, the five of them automatically clustered at the door leading outside. When a person leaves a house, it is only natural to want to depart through the door. However, the disadvantages of this sort of thinking presented themselves all too clearly to the giant's five prisoners as they looked up at the distant shape of the immense door handle.

"How can we turn the handle?" Dilly asked in a whisper. Cam thought that their ordinary voices were probably too soft to wake up the giants, but it seemed right to whisper simply because they were *sneaking*.

"A window would be better," Crobbs said.

The kitchen was in one corner of the house and had

two windows. It was hard to see them from far down on the floor, and with so little light.

"They're closed," Nort concluded.

"If they were open, we'd feel the cool night air," Spinach said. The others stared at her. "I've made a great study of windows and breezes," she explained.

"We could see if any of the other windows in the house are open," Dilly suggested.

This led to an exploration of the house, an endeavor enlivened when Cam and Spinach found out just how loudly a giant could snore. But not one window was open, and the group eventually returned to the kitchen, tired and discouraged.

The great wizard Lex sat in Malison's magic workroom in an overstuffed chair covered with black brocade, drinking hot chocolate from a gold mug and wiggling his sock-clad toes.

Malison's workroom was nicer than Lex's. Well, not nicer so much as better, which didn't surprise him a bit. Lex felt a faint buzzing in his head, but he gave it a shake and the buzzing went away. He stole another look at Malison, who sipped her hot chocolate with dainty malevolence.

Then Lex noticed a slender onyx tube in one corner of the room. "Is that a Corilanus cry-flute?" he asked.

"It is. Do you like it?"

"Oh yes," Lex breathed. He liked everything in this room: the lizard-birds in cages made of bones, the books that snapped at him when he passed the rows of shelves, the scarred blackwood worktable, the desk piled with sinister papers and glimmering knickknacks, the rows of glass vials and jars filled with liquids in each of the seventeen colors of flame, the stuffed basilisk hanging overhead—Lex blushed, thinking of his own alligator—and of course, Malison herself. Malison was very pretty *and* she knew about magic. Lex sighed blissfully. Then he looked around. There was only one thing missing from this marvelous room. "Where's Meg?" he asked.

"She wasn't interested in seeing my workroom," Malison said, watching Lex closely. "She is not like you and me."

"You and me," Lex repeated, feeling a little fuzzy. Lex and Malison. That was a good thought. But what did the sorceress mean about Meg? "She isn't? What are we like?"

Malison pulled her chair closer to Lex's, which wasn't easy to do, since it was made of a single bleak stone. The carvings on the armrests and sides showed an army of hideous beings attacking a city where people screamed and died in terror. Lex peered at the carvings. "What are those creatures?"

"Undead warriors," Malison said. "But you asked a question: 'What are we like?' "

"Oh, right." Lex wondered why he felt so groggy.

And coming up the hall, his legs had been strangely stiff. He reminded himself that he'd walked up a mountain and a lot of stairs today. Plus just being around Malison seemed to have an effect on him.

"We are the Powerful Ones," Malison intoned.

Lex tried to pay attention, but he wasn't sure what his hostess was trying to say. "We are?" he said, puzzled. "Oh, you mean because of the magic."

"Magical greatness isn't an ordinary thing," Malison told him.

Lex took another swallow of his hot chocolate. "No. My father and mother were always saying that. 'Lex,' they told me, 'you're a weird boy. But we love you anyway.' "

" 'Weird'?" Malison said distastefully. "*My* parents cowered at my feet."

Lex was astonished. "*Why?* I mean, I can't imagine my parents doing that." Malison must have had a very odd childhood.

Only a teensy bit exasperated, Malison forged ahead. "Well, maybe not your parents, then. But, Lex—is that really your name?—haven't you ever wanted to wield your vast power out in the world?"

"Wizards don't tell their real names," Lex said primly. Not even to wonderful sorceresses, he thought with a twinge of regret. It just wasn't done.

"Fine. But what about your power? And your inner darkness? Don't you want to set it free? Say, loose it upon an unsuspecting populace?"

"It's just . . ." Lex said, embarrassed. "No, I can't tell you that."

Malison attempted to look sympathetic. "You can, too. I won't laugh."

Lex hesitated. On the one hand, this girl apparently *liked* inner darkness; on the other, Lex had always been one to spill his guts and hope for the best. "I don't think I actually have any inner darkness," he blurted.

"What about your black clothes?" Malison asked, frowning. Then she got a little sarcastic. "Are you sure you aren't an apprentice thief? Perhaps a junior assassin?"

Lex drew himself up in his chair. "I am a wizard," he said with dignity. "But I'm not *mean*." His mind didn't feel quite so fuzzy anymore.

Malison gritted her beautiful teeth and tried again. She waved her hand at the desk. "What's mean about wanting to own the Languid Eye of Toth? Or the Deceptive Dagger of Hee-Kethlan-T'resk? Or even"— she paused dramatically—"the Angled Orb of Nonbeing?"

Lex brightened. "You have all that? Can I see?" He set his nearly empty mug down on top of a pile of extremely expensive books and almost tripped rushing over to Malison's desk, where he lifted each magical artifact, peppering her with questions. "Does it just make people *think* they're in another world? Or are they really *in* another world, at least their spirits, maybe not their bodies? How did you ever get into the Locked Temple of Crenellation? Is this one made of dragon's gold, or regular gold? Did the Priests of Moop let you borrow their ring of power? Do you have to give it back sometime?"

"Lex!" Malison said in a not-at-all-elegant voice.

Startled, Lex put down the object he was holding, a small onyx cup shaped like an ear, complete with a ruby-and-diamond earring. "What?"

"Do you or do you not want to join your magic to mine and help me extend my evil empire?"

"Oh. Is that what you want?" Doing anything with Malison sounded enticing, but evil empires weren't exactly Lex's style. "Well, no. It's very nice of you to ask, though. But I'm on a quest with Meg. When is she coming back, anyway? She likes hot chocolate almost as much as I do."

Malison appeared to be counting to ten under her breath for some reason. "Perhaps she'll join us for breakfast." Malison imitated a smile. "I believe she said she was too tired to join us for dinner."

"I'm tired, too," Lex said. "But I'd like to read some of your books. Or maybe you could show me one of your spells."

Little did he know, Malison told herself with a fair dose of irony. She considered the possibilities. "It's getting late. I'll take you to your room, and then tomorrow morning you can come look through my library."

"All right," Lex said, unaware that his face was now

blue with yellow spots and that butterfly wings were sprouting from the back of his head. "Hey, is that a toe knuckle from a seven-toed ice monster? I've always wanted one of those. Where did you get it?"

But Malison was already out the door, and Lex had to hurry to keep up. As he walked, his face changed back to its usual color. A moment later, the butterfly wings detached themselves from his head and flew away down the hall. "Did you say something?" Lex asked.

"No."

Lex was sure Malison had said something, even if it was under her breath. "You were talking to yourself, weren't you? You did it before, too. On the stairs."

Malison flicked him a look. "You caught me. I was thinking out loud."

"It's not such a bad habit," Lex said kindly, but the sorceress didn't answer. He followed her along two more halls and up a flight of stairs, unaware that halfway up he turned into a pug dog. By the time he reached the door of the room where Malison said he'd be sleeping, he had changed back into a boy. Lex's bark transformed itself abruptly into words. "Something smells funny," he said.

"I'm sure it does," Malison told him, trying to think of another spell. She'd been throwing one trick of magic after another at this wizard boy, and none of them seemed to stick. The best she'd gotten was a bit of a daze and enough of a deafness spell to separate him from his friend, but both had soon faded. Then the spell for canceling out magic had canceled itself out, and the one for total obedience had produced only a mild good cheer, which Malison suspected was mostly Lex's personality.

He seemed to like her, but not slavishly, the way her enchanted guards adored her. Not the way he was supposed to. She didn't want him blushing and stammering; she wanted him in her *thrall*, so when she said "Evil henchman," his only response would be to ask, "How evil?"

Malison scowled. She had turned Lex into a marble statue on the way to her workroom, but it hadn't lasted five minutes. She had barely had time to name the thing *Young Wizard Vanquished* when all of the color had flooded back into Lex's face and hands.

Malison tried a sleep spell, that old standby. But Lex merely yawned.

This was a new experience for Malison, and it made her very unhappy.

16

MEG CLOSED THE DOOR OF HER DUNGEON CELL behind her. When Stefka left, she'd gone off to the right. Down the other way Meg could just see the doors of other cells. Inside one of those dark spaces was Alya, and Alya needed to be let out.

Meg walked slowly along the rough stone corridor, looking into each barred window. She saw nothing in the first or the second, but when she peeked in the third, a ghastly face looked back at her, something yellowish with fangs. Meg shrieked and then hushed herself. The thing whined at her pathetically, but Meg was afraid to let it out. "Sorry," she whispered, moving on to the next door. "Alya?" she said, but no one answered. She checked another cell, and another.

"Who is that?" she heard up ahead. Meg hurried to find the source of the voice. "Alya?" She stopped in front of the right door at last.

Alya stared back at her for a shocked instant before she said, "Meg? Princess—what are *you* doing here?"

Meg hurriedly unlocked the door. "I'm looking for my dragon. I hear Miss Arrogance took your village captive."

"Yes," Alya said shortly, stepping into the dim corridor. The Bandit Queen was thin and dirty, her black hair a tangled mass. "How did you get the key? None of my people have been able to get their hands on one."

"There was this hawk," Meg began, but seeing the look on Alya's face, she interrupted herself. "Never mind. I don't know where anything is, though. I was locked up until just a little while ago. Now I need to find Lex."

"Lex?"

"The wizard boy. He's up there with her."

"That's all she needs, a wizard under her spells." Alya started walking.

"What are you going to do?" Meg asked her.

Alya smirked. "Organize the women in the kitchen, of course. It's something men never seem to expect."

Meg nodded and followed Alya up the dungeon stairs, hoping there wasn't a guard posted at the top.

There was, but he was dozing a bit, though he woke up when Alya attacked. Pretty soon the guard was sitting in his chair again, but this time he was tied to it, and his mouth was full of black cloth ripped from his own shirt.

They nearly ran across another pair of guards as they

looked for the kitchen, but Meg and Alya were able to hide behind a cabinet and a pompous vase full of harpy feathers until the men passed, their torches flickering weirdly.

The next person they met was a servant woman, one of Alya's band. She almost dropped the basket full of black laundry she was carrying. Her mouth went round with astonishment. Then she smiled, hope blossoming in her face. "Alya! It's really you!"

A few minutes later, Alya was holding a midnight meeting in the kitchen with a dozen of her followers and Meg. The women spent the first part of the meeting indignantly describing Malison's demands.

"She wants to bathe in rose water!" one burly woman grumped. "We're half the day picking roses and pulling the petals off."

"*And* the water has to be hot, so we use the stoves to heat it, but that puts us off the dinner schedule—"

"Then she's angry about dinner being late!"

"You call that dinner? Whoever heard of eating candied peacock's eggs?"

"She won't settle for fish and potatoes, not her."

"Why can't she just use a spell to heat the water?"

Alya seemed to understand that the women needed to complain before they could get anything else done. She listened and made noises of sympathy and outrage until everyone had settled down a bit. Then she started a discussion about how to free the villagers from the sorceress.

No one paid the least bit of attention to Meg.

"Excuse me," Meg said finally. "Can I get a black dress? Then I'll be on my way."

Alya remembered her. "This is Meg, also known as the Princess of Greeve, though we try not to hold that against her. She came here with a friend she wants to rescue."

Stefka looked at her more closely. "You! How did you get out?"

"There was this hawk . . ." Meg said, but everyone sort of frowned, and she gave up. "I had a key."

"She let me out, too," Alya said.

"Good girl," Stefka told Meg.

"Now she wants to go up there and find her friend," Alya added.

"A man?" a skinny blond woman asked. The other women chuckled.

"Worse," Alya said, watching Meg. "A wizard."

"A sort of cheery boy with red hair?" a woman who hadn't said anything yet asked.

"That's him!" Meg exclaimed.

"Tell us, Luli," Alya said.

"I take him his towels," Luli said. "He's very nice. Not like her."

"If you could show me," Meg began, but Alya was shaking her head. "You'll have to wait, Meg. If they catch you while we're in the middle of our plan, it'll all fall apart."

"But I don't have time!" Meg cried. "I only have five days, four days now. There's this giant, and this thief—"

A few of the women muttered at the sound of the word "thief." Meg supposed the former bandits were touchy about remarks on their previous trade. "I have to help my friends," Meg explained. "Just like you're doing."

"We'll help you with your wizard," Alya said. "It will be easy once we've gotten to that sorceress."

Meg looked around at the circle of faces: weary, angry women whose everyday lives had been stolen from them, whose fathers and brothers and husbands and sons were under a spell. "All right," she said. "I hope it's a *fast* plan."

"It'll have to be fast," Alya told her. "Someone's going to find that guard we tied up."

"There must be some other way out," Crobbs said hopefully.

The others were silent, standing in the middle of the wide kitchen floor in the near darkness, presumably thinking. Unfortunately, they must not have thought of anything much, because the silence continued, and continued . . .

"There isn't, is there?" Dilly said.

"If we can't open the door, we need someone to open it for us," Cam said slowly.

"They won't do that!" Nort told him.

"They won't know they're doing it," Cam went on.

"Ah," said Nort. "We wait for the door to open and then rush out."

"That's it."

"Has anyone got a better idea?" Dilly asked. "Because the minute that child finds out we're gone, they'll be looking for us."

"We just have to hope her mother opens the kitchen door before Loris gets up." There was another silence as the little group considered the odds of this happening.

"Well," said Nort. "We need to find a good hiding place near the door."

"The cupboard's not close enough," Dilly observed.

"What about that chair?" Spinach asked. It was amazing how a chair could loom, each of its legs bigger than a tree trunk. The night shadows painted it with menace. It was almost enough to make Spinach wish she was back in her tower.

"No," Cam said. "The broom."

"Is that what that is?" Crobbs said.

The broom leaned against the wall beside the door, a thicket of tall straw bristles rising up over their heads toward a handle that was lost in the darkness high above them. "It's the closest thing," Nort said reluctantly.

"It's on the wrong side of the door," Dilly said.

"We'll have to run around the door after it's

opened." Cam didn't sound as if he liked his own plan very much.

They didn't have much of a choice. The five travelers slipped behind the broom, setting up a sort of temporary camp between the wall and the bristle thicket.

The kitchen smelled faintly of the giants' dinner. "Does anybody have anything to eat?" Crobbs said plaintively.

"I saved one of those crumbs," Cam told him. Cam divided the crumb into five pieces. The little group sat on the floor eating the rough giant bread, waiting for dawn and the door to open.

The next morning found Malison slouched on her throne pouting. Every once in a while she would think up an order to give, mostly because she liked seeing the guardsmen run off to fetch whatever it was she wanted this time. Actually, they would go and yell at one of the women servants, who would stalk off in disgust to track down the latest item. None of it pleased Malison, anyway. An ivory fan studded with sapphires—"I said rubies!" A map of Malison's empire—"My part should be bigger. Who drew this?" A single perfect strawberry— "It's not red enough. Take it back!" A book of poems about world conquest—"That's the wrong one!" Some curried mushroom-and-ham on toast—"The curry's too strong!"

Then Bain approached her. "Your Majesty?"

He was really very nice-looking, her chief guard, Malison thought before she remembered she was in a bad mood. "What is it?" she snapped.

"I must inform you that one of the dungeon guards has been overpowered and tied to a chair."

Malison scrambled to sit up. "And the prisoners?"

"The new prisoner is missing. As is Alya."

"What? Didn't you lock them in?" Malison cried. "Didn't you *turn* the *key* in the *lock*?"

"I did, mistress," Bain said miserably. "I don't know what happened."

"Search the fortress!" Malison barked. "Find them before they cause any trouble!"

As Bain hurried away, she called after him, "And keep that princess away from my pet wizard!"

It wasn't long before guards were poking into every corner of the fortress, swords at the ready. They searched the kitchens with extra care, making the women stand to one side in their tidy uniforms. And really, should they have been expected to notice that there was one kitchen maid too many? The problem with bespelled guards is that their minds are always just a little foggy. And the problem with women servants is that they all look alike to a bespelled guard.

Meg stood quietly in the line of servants, watching the guards open each of the cupboards and peer into the largest kettles. Alya was right: they weren't going to see her here. The Bandit Queen wasn't in the kitchen at all.

Her loyal friends had helped her move across the fortress unseen early this morning. Now she waited, motionless, in the perfect spot for vanquishing a sorceress, reflecting on the fact that people expect a fugitive to be too frightened to try anything daring.

Hours passed, and finally a very unhappy Bain made his way back toward Malison's throne room, where one of the youngest guards was feeding the Empress of the Southern Reaches peeled grapes and trying not to cry. Malison noticed his nervousness. She smiled for the first time since she'd settled Lex in her workroom with a stack of magic books earlier that morning. "If you cry, I'll turn you into a lizard."

Her threat was the last straw, of course. The boy gulped and swiped and sniffled, but one tear escaped him and rolled down his newly pale cheek. "Ha!" Malison said, and she chanted a spell. An instant later a small purple lizard scuttled away beneath her throne. Grapes rained down onto the black marble, a gold plate clattering after them, but it was worth it.

One of the guards ran to fetch someone to clean up the mess, and a woman servant soon appeared with a hand broom and dustpan. A moment later Bain returned, more worried than Malison had ever seen him. His men filed into the hall in silent ranks behind him and arrayed themselves properly off to either side of the throne. "I'm terribly sorry, Empress," Bain said, "but we haven't been able to find the prisoners. Perhaps they've left the fortress altogether."

"Perhaps I need a new chief guard!" Malison hissed. Bain bowed his head, waiting, which made Malison more angry than ever. "Look at me!" she cried, and he raised his head again. "Tell me how lovely I am," she said in a nicer voice.

"You're as beautiful as a sunrise," Bain began. He had obviously been through this before.

Malison's latest frown softened a little. "And?"

"And even more beautiful than a sunset," Bain went on.

"Are you saying a sunrise is better-looking than a sunset?" Malison said, narrowing her eyes.

"I'm saying . . ." Bain paused, trying to figure out just what he was saying. "That the evening sun is ashamed to remove its light from illuminating the glory of your countenance, while the morning sun rejoices in being able to see your face once more after the long, dark night."

A faint snort came from the woman who was picking up the last of the grapes. Unfortunately, Malison heard her, and a green lizard skittered to join the purple one underneath the throne. The grapes, the gold dish, the hand broom, and the dustpan all fell to the floor in a small symphony of thuds and clatters.

"After the long, dark night?" Malison repeated as

though nothing had interrupted her conversation with Bain. "Ah. That explains it." She sank back on her throne, pleased, then flicked a finger at the guard nearest Bain. "You, what do you say I'm more beautiful than?"

The man took a deep breath, thinking of that lizard, not to mention Malison's wonderfulness. "You're more beautiful than the snowfall."

"And you?" Malison pointed to another.

"More beautiful than a flower garden."

Down the line she went.

"More beautiful than the stars!"

"Than an emerald! With rubies and diamonds on top!"

This was hard to follow, but the next man tried. "Than a unicorn!"

"Than a painting in a gold frame!"

"Than a fish!"

Malison paused. "A *fish*?"

The guard stuttered. "I used to b-be a fisherman. B-b-before I came to w-work for you. And I used to say there was no p-prettier sight—"

"A *fish*?" Malison said again. Another lizard scurried beneath her throne. It was gray.

Malison stared fiercely around at her guards, all of whom took an adoring yet frightened step back. "I'll just have to locate the prisoners myself," she said, kicking her foot petulantly.

17

THE MORNING LIGHT SLIPPED INTO THE GIANTS' kitchen like a spy, where it discovered five tiny people sleeping in awkward heaps behind the broom bristles. Half an hour later, the sound of giant footsteps somewhere in the house woke Nort. He shook the others softly. "Get ready," he whispered.

Whoever was awake didn't come into the kitchen at first—they must have gone into the bathroom. Long, tense minutes passed before footsteps clomped down the hall toward the waiting humans. The broom blocked their view, but Nort suspected the approaching giant was Lorgley, since he walked more heavily than his wife and daughter.

To everyone's delight, the giant headed straight for the door, turning the huge handle easily and swinging the door open.

Dilly was already in motion, with Nort right behind

her. Spinach and Cam rushed after them, and Crobbs brought up the rear. But as fast as they ran, Lorgley was faster. The door shut with a horrendous boom. They all fell down behind it, bumping their heads and elbows together.

Dilly was the first to speak. "If he comes back, he'll open the door and hit us with it." No one argued with her. They got up and trudged back to their hiding place, thoroughly disheartened.

"This isn't going to work," Cam said. "I'm sorry."

"Now, you don't know that," Nort said staunchly. "Sometimes people leave doors open longer, or stand in the doorway talking."

"That's true," Dilly said.

Nort smiled. Dilly didn't often agree with him.

"But then there's Loris," Spinach pointed out. "What if she catches us? Or steps on us? Do you think giants pay attention to what's on the floor?"

No one answered Spinach, though Nort and Dilly exchanged a long-suffering look, tired of the girl's questions—especially the ones that evoked images of being squashed by giant feet.

"We have to try again," Crobbs said at last in the silence, and of course he was right.

They were so busy concentrating on waiting for Lorgley to come back from outside that when Kitty Comprost bustled into the kitchen, she surprised them all. Especially when she picked up the broom to sweep. Startled, Nort grabbed the bristle he'd been leaning against, only to be lifted into the air and shoved around the kitchen with the dizzying, dangerous thrusts of Kitty's broom.

Behind her the others froze, wishing they could disappear. There weren't any good hiding places within reach, and besides, they were watching Nort with horrified fascination. Nort was jarred by every stroke of the broom against the floor and seemed perilously close to being shaken loose.

Then Kitty looked down and saw the four of them standing there. She screamed good and loud before she started slapping at them with the broom. "SHOO! SHOO!" she shouted. "NASTY LITTLE THINGS!"

The four remaining humans ran every which way, racing to avoid Kitty's angry broom. Swerving and skidding, they led the giant woman in a mad dance around the room. One of her blows caught Dilly with the edge of the bristles, and Dilly slid hard across the kitchen after one terrifying upside-down glimpse of Nort's face. Kitty spun about, trying to swat the five of them at once.

Something thumped out in the hall, and Loris burst into the kitchen. "MOMMY, MY DOLLIES ARE GONE!" She stopped, flabbergasted. "MY DOLLIES! STOP, MOMMY, STOP!" Loris grabbed her mother's arm just before Kitty could whack Cam a good one.

"NO!" Kitty cried, but in that instant's pause, Nort jumped clear of the broom. Almost immediately, the giant's wife began swinging the broom again despite Loris's protests. Seeing her mother had no intention of stopping her wild broomwork, Loris decided to rescue her dollies one at a time. She started crawling around the floor after them, ducking her mother's broom and stretching her hands out now here, now there to grasp the five humans who darted between her fingers. Loris nearly caught Dilly, who was slowing a little and wondering how much longer she could keep running. It was only lunging behind a chair leg that saved Dilly for a few seconds more.

Then the door opened, and Lorgley Comprost stepped into the kitchen. "WHAT'S GOING ON IN HERE?" he boomed.

The door was still open. *"The door!"* Cam yelled at the others. *"Run!"* Suddenly all five of them changed direction, running straight for the door. Except Spinach, who was Loris's most important target. She had to zigzag inventively to keep away from the giant child. Loris slid across the floor on her belly, her fingers brushing Spinach's back. "ROSALINA LILIANA!" Loris wailed. "MOMMY, THEY'RE GETTING AWAY!"

Lorgley had been trying to calm his wife. On hearing his daughter's words, he leaped to close the door, but his prisoners raced outside before he could get there. He tried to go after them—and so did Loris. In her haste to recapture Spinach, Loris tripped her father. She simply sat down hard, but Lorgley fell flat on his back with a giant crash. "KITTY!" he bellowed. His wife hurried to help him up.

The three giants rushed out the door, but there was no sign of the little humans, only the nodding of daisies and snapdragons in the early summer breeze.

Bain looked hopeful for the first time that day when he heard Malison planned to aid him in his search. "You'll use magic to find the prisoners, Empress?"

"What else would I use?" Malison drummed her fingers on the arm of her throne. It wasn't the kind of question anyone actually felt inclined to answer.

Malison began to stand up, but just then Alya's hiding place was revealed. Two slim hands appeared from behind the throne and a dagger crossed Malison's neck, holding her in place. Alya rose over the sorceress like an angry dragon. "Take the spell off my brother and the others!" she commanded.

The initial alarm cleared from Malison's face far too soon. "I've found one of your missing prisoners," she told Bain spitefully.

Alya tightened her hold on Malison. "I said, take the spell off! Or it will have to stop when you die."

"But you don't *know* that will happen, do you?" Malison asked, finally addressing her captor.

Bain took a step closer. "Stay back!" his sister cried,

her voice and face showing an edge of desperation only when she spoke to him.

Malison laughed. "A dagger isn't much good against a sorceress. You should know that by now. Go ahead—cut my throat."

Bain was still moving in. Frantic now, Alya tried to hurt the sorceress, but Malison was already saying a spell, and the blade suddenly went useless and bendy. The sorceress spat out a second spell, searing words that made Alya fall sideways even as Bain finally leaped for the throne, determined to protect Malison against his sister.

"Very good, Chief Guard," Malison said. "Bring her where I can see her."

Bain dragged Alya's limp body out in front of the throne.

"Hmm," Malison said. "The woman really should die. But I have something better in mind." She was still smarting from the failure of her statue spell on Lex yesterday. "Bain, hold her so she's standing up. You there"—she indicated another guard—"put her hand around her dagger as if she were about to strike." The guards hurried to obey, and after a few more orders, Alya was posed exactly right. Malison performed the spell. This time it worked. Malison sighed happily, admiring the black marble statue. "I'll call it *The Assassin's Failure*," she said as she stood up. "Put it over there. I'm going to find that princess."

✦

Meg hadn't been very impressed by Alya's plan, but she hadn't wanted to say so. There had been some promising talk about putting sleepy herbs in the guards' suppers, but when all was said and done, getting Alya close to Malison turned out to be the entire plan. From what Meg had seen of that sorceress, it might not be enough. Before everyone had gone back to bed, Meg asked Luli to tell her where Lex was, but Luli changed the subject.

In the morning, Meg was assigned to help dust the furniture in one of the lower hallways, and she couldn't stand it another minute. When the other girl went off to get more water, Meg slipped away. She had hidden a couple of black towels under her skirt the night before as if they were extra petticoats. Now she pulled them out, folded them neatly, and carried them up the stairs, pretending she had a destination.

Meg flinched whenever she saw a guard coming, but she reminded herself that she was practically invisible. She kept walking, eyes lowered. The fortress guards she passed didn't give her a second glance.

Of course, Meg couldn't help wishing Malison's fortress had fewer rooms, let alone fewer halls and stairways. She spent the morning looking in door after door after door, but she didn't find Lex. She found rooms full of weapons in stacks: swords and spears and truncheons and maces and regular crossbows and larger arbalests like the one Lex had transformed for her a few days ago, back before they'd entered the enchanted forest. She found a room all hung with black bats that opened their eyes blearily when the light fell across them. There was a room with a single pedestal in the middle, a tiny gold box sitting atop it, and another room that, while it was filled with glass models of palaces, smelled like barbecued chicken. Then Meg came across a swathe of dozens of guest rooms made up with black satin quilts. It wasn't as if Malison had many friends to come and stay in those rooms, Meg thought as she marched up the next stairway.

"You there!" A guard hailed her, and Meg froze.

"Yes, sir?" she asked in her best innocent servant voice.

The guard was tall and a little plump, his black armor straining around his belly. His kindly face didn't seem to match his current career, and Meg wondered what he used to do before Malison's spell came along to change his life. "Have you seen any escaped prisoners?" the man asked.

"Not today, sir," she replied.

"Very well. Go on, then."

Cam had been in love with plants for a long time, but today he was feeling especially appreciative of daisies and snapdragons. *Giant* daisies and snapdragons, their tangle of leaves and stems providing very good cover for five small humans trying to hide from a family of giants.

Lorgley and Kitty gave up the search after peering into the foliage for five or ten minutes. If it weren't for Loris, the escaped prisoners could have moved on immediately. The giant child poked about in the flowers and shrubs with seemingly endless patience.

She nearly caught Crobbs, too. The tall boy almost gave himself away when a giant bee landed on his head. But Cam grabbed his arm and said "No!" in such a fierce whisper that Crobbs managed to hold still, though he was shaking all over. The bee soon concluded that Crobbs didn't have any nectar in his hair and flew off with a tremendous throaty buzzing sound. Crobbs dropped to his knees, slapping at his hair to brush the pollen out of it. "Well done," Cam said as Loris moved on to another stretch of plants.

A little while later, Kitty saved them by calling her daughter in for breakfast.

"BUT I'M LOOKING FOR MY DOLLIES!" Loris exclaimed.

"YOU CAN LOOK AGAIN AFTER BREAKFAST."

"MO-O-O-TH-ER!" came the giant child's despairing cry.

"LORIS, I'M COUNTING TO FIVE. GET YOUR BOTTOM IN THIS KITCHEN THIS MINUTE! ONE . . . TWO . . . THREE . . ."

"I'M COMING," Loris said sulkily, and she went in the house, slamming the door behind her to further express her indignation. From within, they could hear Loris getting in trouble for slamming the door.

"*Now* they open the windows," Nort remarked.

"Come on," Dilly said. "We have to cover as much ground as possible before that girl finishes her breakfast."

18

DILLY AND THE OTHER FOUR ESCAPEES CLIMBED out of the flowerbed into a narrow groove of dirt that marked the edge of a field of green grass that the giants apparently grew in front of their home for decorative purposes. It was slow going. Dirt that would have seemed fairly smooth to the giants was a jumble of clods large enough to trip smaller folk. "This is worse than walking on that rug," Cam said. "On the other hand," he added, "we're free!"

"Free is good," said Dilly, "but how are we going to get *down*?"

"We could catch a bird and fly down," Crobbs said.

"A bird might eat us," Spinach said. "In this place, we're not much bigger than a worm." A few minutes later her point was proven when they came across an actual worm.

"Blech!" said Crobbs.

"Blech is right," Nort told him. The worm didn't seem particularly interested in them, but it was just so big and round and *gooshy*-looking.

"Worms are good for the garden," Cam told the other four. But Dilly noticed he didn't get any closer to this worm than the rest of them. The travelers moved a little faster until they were well past it. Then Spinach thought of half a dozen questions about worms. Cam answered every single one.

How he could be so patient was beyond Dilly. "Why do you ask so many questions?" Dilly said, trying not to snap when she said it.

"Because," Spinach said, surprised, "I don't know anything. It's hard to know things when you're in a tower." She swept her hand in a circle, pointing all around them. "I want to know *everything*."

"Huh," Dilly said, feeling a lot less irritated all of a sudden.

Meg was peeping into what felt like the hundredth room of the morning with not a single sign of Lex's ever having been there when two guards came around the corner and looked right at her. She ran the other way, but three guards appeared ahead of her and she was surrounded. "Come along," one of the guards said gruffly. "She wants you in the great hall."

So once more Meg found herself standing in front of

Malison's throne, wishing she were somewhere else. "How did you find me?" Meg asked.

Malison didn't bother to answer. "Have you seen my latest creation?"

"Creation?"

"Over there." The Empress of the Southern Reaches pointed.

"It looks like—oh, Alya," Meg said, dismayed.

"I *thought* you would appreciate my work. Well, my work . . ." Malison laughed. "That statue's just a trifle. I'm really in the business of conquest."

"I know, I know," Meg said, "the Southern Reaches."

"Simply a beginning," Malison said. "Later this week, say, on Thursday after I've had a nice lunch, I'm going to start on the Northern Reaches. The Kingdom of Greeve seems like an obvious choice, for example."

"It does not!" Meg cried.

"Do you have a mommy and daddy?" Malison cooed. "Too bad you won't be there to see the castle fall down on their heads and their people join my army of servants."

"You mean slaves. Servants get paid. They even get days off sometimes," Meg said bitterly.

Malison stroked her chin in a villainous gesture her evil-regent uncle had taught her. It wasn't quite the same without a black goatee, but you can't have everything. "Days off? No. I believe we may actually agree on something, Princess. My servants will henceforth be referred to as slaves. Bain, make a note of it."

"Yes, mistress," Bain said with a deep bow.

He was such a *minion*! Meg made the kind of face usually reserved for three-week-old meat. "You've *ruined* him."

"He's an excellent chief guard," Malison said sweetly. "But enough small talk. Before I punish you for escaping, I have a few questions. First of all, who helped you? Was it my servants? My slaves, rather? I might have to start fresh there."

"Of course not! I stole this dress from those stupid women," Meg said.

"And the key? Who gave you the key?"

Meg sighed. "While I was in the enchanted forest, there was this hawk—"

Malison pursed her lips. "I can see you're going to lie about it. Very well. We'll skip ahead to the part where I terrorize you a bit before I send you to your doom." She examined her scarlet-dagger fingernails. "I *could* suspend you from the highest tower, where you would slowly starve to death, burned and pummeled by the sun and the rain respectively."

"You could," Meg said with more bravado than she felt.

"Or I could have my black horses drag you up and down the mountain in a barrel filled with nails. That's always a hit."

"Nails pointing in or out?" Meg said pertly.

"Puh-lease," Malison said, and continued. "I could

assign a minion to tickle you until you choke on your own laughter." She paused. "But that's just a little too cute."

Meg took a step toward Malison, not feeling diplomatic in the least. "Blah, blah, blah. What are you really going to do? Turn me into a statue, like Alya?"

Malison leaned forward in her throne and said tauntingly, "No. She wasn't a princess. *You* are a princess."

"True." Meg waited for the sorceress to get to the point.

Malison was too pleased with herself to notice Meg's sarcasm. *"I,"* the sorceress said with a dramatic flourish of her hands, "am going to feed you to my dragon."

Meg's eyes grew wide. Laddy! She forced her mouth to stay still. "You have a dragon?"

"I do," Malison said proudly.

"Not—not a dragon," Meg said, and her voice trembled. She wasn't certain whether to laugh or cry. She couldn't know for sure, but she could hope.

"Oh, indeed," Malison said. "My gorgeous, slithery, hungry pet. Bain!"

"Yes, mistress?" Those seemed to be the only two words he knew, Meg thought irritably.

"Take this girl and throw her to the dragon."

Bain's forehead wrinkled as if he were trying to remember something, but all he said was, "Yes, mistress."

"Just a minute!" Meg said. "I have a question for you, Your Evilness."

"A last request? Go ahead."

"What have you done with Lex?"

"Why, he's my new best friend," Malison said. "He's going to help me with my conquests."

"He wouldn't do that!"

The black-haired girl didn't bother to argue. She simply watched, smiling, as Meg was dragged away to die in time-honored princess fashion.

For Cam and the others, freedom mostly meant hiding from Loris, who spent the morning searching the flowerbeds for them, but ranged farther afield after lunch. At last evening came and the giant child went in for her supper and bedtime. The five travelers crossed another stretch of grass in the twilight and camped out.

The next morning, after an uneasy night between a mammoth elm tree and a stone wall, they woke up to find that Spinach's hair was three times longer than she was. Braiding it helped, but their packs were variously lying where the giant had taken them prisoner or tucked away in Loris's bedroom drawers. Spinach had to wrap her braid around her waist so many times she practically waddled when she walked.

There was no breakfast. Bruised from the previous few days' adventures and hungrier than they had ever

been in their lives, the five companions sat in a little circle arguing about what to do next.

"We need food," Cam said immediately. Dilly could
hear Crobbs's stomach growling to her left and Nort's
stomach growling to her right. Her own stomach, hearing the noise, soon joined the chorus.

"We need to find out how the giant gets down," Nort
put in. "So we can go home."

"Maybe it's magic," Dilly said.

"Or there's a door, or an invisible stairway, or something," Nort told her. Dilly resisted the urge to point out
that if the stairway was truly invisible, Nort wouldn't be
able to see it. Everyone was disheartened enough as it
was.

"We should catch a bird," Crobbs insisted.

Finally they came to an agreement: Cam and Dilly
and Spinach would journey behind the house to find out
if the giants had a vegetable garden where they could get
something to eat, while Nort and Crobbs would climb
up the elm tree and look out over the giants' land to see
if there was any sign of a way down. After that, Nort
promised, he would help Crobbs try to catch a bird.

"Don't get lost," Nort told the other three by way of
farewell.

Dilly had no intention of getting lost. "We won't,"
she said with asperity. "We'll stick close to the house and
come back the same way."

To the relief of the three explorers, Loris didn't resume her search for them today. Dilly wasn't sure whether the giant child had lost interest or Loris's mother had told her not to look anymore. Either way, it was one less thing to worry about. But Spinach brought up a new worry. "If there isn't a vegetable garden, what will we do?" she asked. "Will we have to eat bugs? Won't they taste nasty?"

"We'll have to go back inside and find food in that kitchen," Cam said.

This was so unthinkable that they were quiet for a while afterward. They finished crossing the grass and traveled along in single file next to the house. They didn't meet any more worms, although they saw several pill bugs and a number of determined-looking ants. They nearly bumped into a stinkbug, too. "Watch out for the skunk," Cam informed the others. Dilly laughed, but Spinach stared at them, bewildered. She hadn't had much practice with jokes, either, Dilly realized as Cam explained about skunks.

It was nearly noon when they came to the back corner of the giants' house and peeked around it. At first they couldn't see anything but more towering trees and bushes, but then Cam pointed. "There!" he said. "Those are cornstalks!"

"Food," Dilly said happily.

"I don't like corn," Spinach said.

"There will be other things," Cam said, grinning.

"Tomatoes, squash, beans—lots of good growing things."

"I don't like vegetables," Spinach said. "I like bread and butter."

"Perhaps we'll find a bread-and-butter tree," Cam said. Spinach looked at him doubtfully for a moment before she realized he was joking and smiled. There was hope for her yet, Dilly thought with a smile of her own.

"If you're hungry enough, I suspect you'll be able to swallow a vegetable or two," Dilly told the girl.

"I suppose," Spinach replied, though she didn't sound convinced that beans and squash were any better to eat than rocks and dirt.

Meg waited till she was clear of the great hall before she asked Bain, "What does this dragon look like, the one that's going to eat me? Is it one of those extra-toothy green dragons from the Eastern Seas? Or a black ripper from the Islands of Konsi?"

"I'm not supposed to talk to you," Bain said, and that was all he would say. He and three other guards marched Meg silently through the halls of the fortress to an outer courtyard with a small iron gate on the opposite side.

Those few minutes were far too long for Meg.

What if she was wrong?

What if she was right?

The beasts weren't housed in the main fortress but in a special building behind it. Meg could smell the building before they reached it, and then she could hear it:

the shrieks and growls and barks of Malison's inhuman prisoners.

Bain hurried Meg through the menagerie, but she still managed to glimpse a number of its inhabitants. There were creatures she'd heard of, like griffins and grendels and chapalus and firebirds, and others she hadn't, like the giant blue snake that was turning into a tree, or the furry thing that flew around its cage on spinning rainbow wings howling like death. "Are the cages reinforced with magic?" she asked nervously after a stomach-face threw itself against the bars, trying to attack them as they passed.

Of course Bain wouldn't answer.

There was no sign of a dragon in the main menagerie. Meg and her guards traveled beyond it through several twisting corridors that led to a rough stone flight of stairs. Down they went, and then down again, this time along a tunnel. Besides the fact that they were descending, the dampness of the air told Meg that they were underground. But gradually the tunnel rose, and after another long walk, Meg could see a door ahead of them. Bain stopped, reaching for his keys. The lock seemed rusty, as if the door were seldom used. "In there," Bain said, gesturing.

Meg didn't have time to think. She stepped through the door and heard it slam shut behind her. In front of her was a walkway followed by open space. Meg forced herself to move forward, and she peered out cautiously into a large underground chamber.

Her first thought was that the room was full of gold and rubies. Then suddenly the gold and rubies moved, and Meg could see a dragon. *Her* dragon. She was so overjoyed to find him at last that she completely forgot she should be relieved, since seeing him also meant she wasn't on the verge of being eaten. "Laddy!" Meg cried.

19

THE DRAGON LIFTED HIS HEAD. LADDY WAS much bigger than he had been the last time she'd seen him, and he was so beautiful he really should be posing for a knight's shield, with his deep red back like a tumble of roses and his sides shimmering with scales like the coins piled up around the cave. Laddy lay upon a heap of gold and jewels, completely surrounded by casks of treasure goblets, filigreed silver ceremonial armor, ornamental headdresses covered with pearls, and spills of necklaces glittering like letters from a rich and forgotten alphabet. Everything shone in the torchlight, and someone other than Meg might have been tempted to dive off the ledge just to be able to touch the treasure as he died breaking his neck on the golden bust of an ancient king.

But all Meg could think about was Laddy. He wasn't

answering, and at first she wondered if he had lost the ability to speak in her mind. *Laddy?* she said again.

Oh, it's you, came the voice in her head. Meg's dragon could still speak, but he wasn't very happy to see her.

I've been looking for you, Meg said. There didn't seem to be a way down. *Can you help me?*

What do you want? Laddy asked.

Get me down so we can talk.

We can talk like this.

"Can you understand me when I talk out loud?" Meg asked. It was something she'd been wanting to know.

Laddy looked at her for a moment without answering. Finally he said, *It's harder.*

I see. Meg sat on the edge of the overhang, which she suspected had been designed just so people could be pushed off it. She supposed she was lucky Bain hadn't come in and given her a push, since it was quite a long way down. *Don't you want to hear how I found you?*

Go ahead.

Meg sighed. *Are you mad at me?*

He didn't answer.

Laddy?

Yes.

I came to say I'm sorry. And to find out if you were all right.

You didn't visit me anymore, he grumbled.

I know.

You promised.

I did promise, she told him.

I had to sleep in the barn.

That's not good.

With the cows.

Meg suppressed an inner grin, he sounded so woeful about the cows. *Oh dear.*

And you promised me a name, the young dragon reminded her.

I've been working on that, actually.

Laddy couldn't help asking, *Really? Like what?*

Well, Lex and Dilly were helping me, but we couldn't think of anything good enough. Not yet, anyway. Meg told him some of the names they'd thought of, and why they wouldn't do. Laddy laughed, especially when she told him about Gariloon.

How did you end up here? Meg asked.

Laddy sat up on his haunches. *I wanted to find my mother's treasure. I found her cave on the mountain, but the gold was gone.*

I guess it should *have been your gold,* Meg said, realizing this for the first time. So Laddy hadn't just been running away—he had been looking for his dragonly heritage.

And when I thought hard, when I pictured the gold, I could sort of smell it, off to the south.

Dragon magic, Meg said, impressed and bemused. She'd been busy thinking about her quest for days, but Laddy had had his own quest all along.

So I followed the smell, and I met some people along the way—

Also some sausages, Meg said reprovingly.

Laddy snickered. *Sausages, too. And I came to a village. But it was empty and I could smell the gold up in the fortress, so I went there and talked to a sorceress.*

Malison, Meg said with ill-concealed distaste. It galled her to think that Laddy had communicated with that despicable girl.

She's nice. She gave me my mother's gold and jewels and her own treasures, too, and said I could guard them for her. And she promised— Laddy stopped.

What?

Never mind.

You can tell me. What else did she promise?

Laddy turned his black-and-gold eyes on her. *She promised me princesses to eat.*

But I'm a princess!

There was an awkward silence before Laddy said, *I know. She said they're what dragons are* supposed *to eat.*

Meg laughed. *She doesn't know, does she?*

What doesn't she know?

It's the same way I like custard best, but Cam prefers ginger cookies, Meg explained.

What are you talking about?

I'm talking about how you like sausages best.

Sausages are wonderful, Laddy agreed.

Well, there you have it, Meg said. *That girl doesn't know everything, even if she acts like she does.*

No. She doesn't know we're friends, does she?

She never would have sent me to see you if she had.

Laddy was silent for a moment. *So you're sorry? About everything?*

Very, Meg said.

That's good, Laddy told her contentedly.

When Nort and Crobbs started their climb up the elm tree, they chose the side away from the house in case anyone should look out and see them. The elm tree had nice, rough bark. That and their small size made it fairly easy to climb up the tree.

Nort climbed higher and higher, getting better at it as he went. He nearly lost his footing when he came across a line of ants traveling swiftly across the elm's trunk, but he quickly got over his surprise and moved past the ant highway without any mishap.

In fact, Nort soon found out that the bark was crawling with insects, all of them far too large for comfort. He saw a ladybug, four tan moths, two striped beetles, several gnats, and a fuzzy spider, not to mention more ants, before he caught up with Crobbs, who was perched like a bizarre little bird on top of an enormous branch just where it jutted out from the tree. "We need to go higher," Crobbs said.

Nort looked down at the circle of grass below them. Off to the sides, their view was blocked by leaves. "Sure."

They passed two more branches before they stopped to rest. "Higher," Crobbs said.

The third time they stopped, a squirrel came racing madly up the tree past them. Strangely enough, the squirrel was normal-sized. A second later, that squirrel was followed by a giant squirrel, a gray-furred monster twice as long as Nort was tall. The two squirrels were gone before Nort and Crobbs even had time to react.

"Who do you think that was?" Crobbs said at last.

"Frist, maybe. The lieutenant was more of a gray color. That one was reddish-brown."

"Do you think he'll get away?"

"Maybe he'll find a crack to hide in," Nort said dubiously. He couldn't help but be a little grateful that the giant squirrel hadn't noticed him and Crobbs.

Behind the giants' house, Dilly, Cam, and Spinach made their way from one bush to another, trying to get to the vegetable garden without being seen by inquisitive eyes. When they finally reached it, Cam stood looking up at the cornstalks for so long that Dilly and Spinach had to poke him to get him moving again.

"We need to find something that's close to the ground and easy to carry," Dilly said.

"Exactly," Cam said. "Let's not bother digging for root vegetables, either." He pulled a small folding knife from his pocket. "Fortunately, we've got this."

Spinach giggled. "You don't want to drag an entire ear of corn back to the elm tree?"

"If Dilly will climb up there and bring one down, I'll carry it all by myself with one hand," Cam said with mock solemnity.

"That's not funny," Dilly said, shuddering at the thought of herself at the top of a giant cornstalk.

They explored the garden for likely dinner prospects, tromping up and down the rows. When the three of them came around a bend next to the bush beans, they dropped right into a mud puddle. By the time they had struggled out, yelling, their legs and arms and faces were covered with muck. "Ptheh," Spinach said, spitting dirt out of her mouth. The outside loops of braid around her waist had turned from yellow to brown.

A few rows later, they came to a puddle of clear water and cleaned themselves off as best they could. Then it was time to gather some food. "I wish I still had my pack," Dilly said, eyeing the plants and vegetables speculatively.

In the end, they bypassed the carrots, the corn, and the turnips, settling on beans and chunks of squash and cabbage that Cam hacked off with his knife.

"Don't make the hole so square!" Dilly told him.

"Why not?"

"We want them to think it was birds or bugs, not us!"

So Cam roughed up the edges of the hole where he'd cut out the squash meat. He looked over at Spinach. The ravenous girl had apparently changed her mind about vegetables once she'd discovered a newly fallen cherry tomato. Spinach held her prize in both hands, taking great bites of it and dripping juice onto her already muddy clothes. She caught Cam's eyes, smiling redly. "It's good!" she said. Spinach ripped off a piece of her tomato, holding it out to Cam.

Cam shook his head. "I'm busy."

"You're silly," Spinach proclaimed. "Both of you should be carrying food back in your stomachs, not just in your hands."

Dilly stopped what she was doing. "Good idea. Why carry food we can eat now?" So the three of them feasted on squash and tomato. Spinach's face when she tried the first bite of squash was a study, but the girl must not have found it so bad, since she ate every bit.

"Have you eaten very many kinds of vegetables before?" Dilly asked.

"No," Spinach said with her mouth full of squash.

"That explains it," Dilly told Cam.

Soon they were pleasantly full, and they went to work packing up food to take back to the others. They used large leaves to wrap their plunder, tearing some of the leaves into long strips for tying their packets together and hanging them over their shoulders.

They were nearly ready to go when Cam saw a snail crawling slowly along. Not that it was scary, but it *was* nearly knee-high in this place. "I hate snails," Cam said.

"Why?" Spinach asked. "Is it because they're squishy?"

She drew in her breath to ask another question, but Cam was already explaining. "They chew up the garden plants. They leave awful ragged holes in everything."

Dilly and Spinach burst out laughing.

"What?" Cam looked from one girl to the other.

"So do we."

Spinach poked Dilly. "Yesterday you were a toy. Today you're a garden pest."

The three of them gathered up the food and started back around the house for the elm tree. Then Cam said, "Did you hear that?" just as two crows burst into the air above the garden, cawing and fighting.

Meg had a little trouble convincing Laddy that Malison was a bad person. *She made everyone in the village into slaves!* Meg explained for the third time. The first time, Laddy had asked, *What's a slave?*

Now he said again, *But I have my mother's gold back, and that's all I want.*

Meg decided to get tough. *You don't really have it back. The gold is Malison's.*

It is not.

She's just letting you touch it.

That's not true! Laddy said, stung.

It's like you're her guard dog. Only you're her guard dragon.

I happen to live here, Laddy said. *With my gold.*

Meg went on relentlessly, *And what do you think would happen if you tried to take your treasure somewhere else?*

She—I don't know. She might not be very happy about it, Laddy admitted.

When she told me about you, she didn't say, 'Oh, there's a neighborly dragon watching his gold, and so he's keeping an eye on my treasures while he's at it.' She called you her pet.

Laddy was silent.

She has a bunch of other pets, you know.

Laddy surprised her by saying, *Wasn't I your pet?*

Maybe a little. When you were more of a baby and needed my help. But now—look at you. You belong to yourself. Meg paused, realizing something else. *You should probably name yourself, too. You don't need me for that.*

But you'll help me?

Of course. I told you I would.

And Malison really is evil?

I wish she weren't, but yes. She is. Meg was reluctant to tell Laddy her biggest fear, but it might help him understand. *She says she's going to conquer Greeve and kill my parents.*

She can't do that! Laddy told her, shocked. *Your father scratched my head once.* He gave an angry little roar. Fire flashed across the treasure chamber, luckily missing Meg, who threw herself sideways.

So, Laddy said when he had caught his breath and Meg had sat up, *what do you want me to do? Besides not eat you, I mean?*

20

NORT AND CROBBS CLIMBED TO AN ASTONISHING height before they stopped again. Nort was glad he wasn't Dilly at this moment, but looking down was still a nerve-racking endeavor. "This should work," he said.

"Out there, you mean." Crobbs gestured along the branch they were sitting on. The elm's trunk had made a good path upward, but they would have to get closer to the ends of the branches to be able to see anything useful past the thick bunches of leaves.

"We could split up," Nort said. "I'll go over on the other side."

"Stay away from giant squirrels," Crobbs said. Nort couldn't tell if the other boy was joking or not, so he just nodded and crept around the trunk toward the next branch up. Keeping an eye out for squirrels, Nort made his way along the branch, which was gratifyingly thick at first, but eventually started to skinny and fork. Then Nort straddled the smaller branch he had chosen and scooted himself forward awkwardly. At last he got so far that the thinner branches swayed and dipped beneath him. Nort backed up a bit and stood, anchoring himself between two whiplike branches as he surveyed the giants' house and land.

Except for a few leaves in his way, leaves as big as Nort, he could see pretty well. The house was off to his left, a little lower than the treetop he was in. Straight ahead he could see a stone well behind the house. It had a little triangular roof like a hat. He could just glimpse the edge of the vegetable garden. The rest of it was hidden behind the house. The sight made him wonder how Dilly and the others were doing. Beyond the well and down a hill, Nort could see the top of another house. More giants. He didn't know what he had expected to see—a stairway topped by a stone arch marked with the word "Belowlands"? He turned to go back to where Crobbs would be waiting for him.

Nort heard the sound before he felt the impact, a whirring of wind followed by a heavy weight hitting his branch. He fell forward, grabbing the bark, and looked wildly over his shoulder into the eyes of a great black beast. He was just recognizing it as a giant crow when the creature pecked at him with a curious beak, stabbing at his leg. "Go away!" Nort yelled. The crow poked him more carefully the second time, apparently startled by the noise Nort made. Then it began snatching at Nort, trying to pull him loose.

Frantic, Nort scrambled forward toward the tree trunk. The crow grabbed the back of his shirt with its beak, and this time Nort lost his balance. He fell down, down, down. He banged against a branch and put out his hands to grab whatever he could, but he was caught out of midair by huge claws and jerked upward. Nort dangled painfully from the crow's claws as the bird's wings loomed over him, flapping hugely to keep them both aloft.

Nort didn't mean to look down, but he did, and his stomach lurched. The crow was flying over the giants' house, and now over the vegetable garden. Soon they would be past the back wall and the next house, on and on, going who knows where?

Then something went wrong as a dark blur came out of the air and tried to grab Nort away from the crow. Nort tilted his head. Another crow. They were fighting over him!

The first crow dove and swerved, but the other came after it in an instant. Nort and his crow swooped and looped, but the second crow didn't give up. Cawing their anger, the two great birds flew up and over and around the giants' house.

After a particularly brilliant sally by the second crow, Nort's lost its grip just the tiniest bit. Without thinking, Nort wiggled free—and fell, shooting headfirst down through air, losing his stomach and his breath, then landing roughly and suddenly in some kind of plant.

He slowly opened his eyes. One of the crows was coming at him again, but the other cut it off, and away the two of them flew, still quarreling. Nort saw that he was still very high up, with green on every side. Next to him was a large green object crowned with what looked like yellow hair. Nort had lived on a farm when he was younger, and he finally recognized what had happened. He had landed on top of one of the corn plants.

Nort breathed out and in, out and in for what seemed like the first time in days before he started to make his way down the cornstalk, listening with one ear for the return of the crows.

He thought he was imagining things at first when he heard voices below him. "Nort! Are you all right?"

Nort tumbled down the last stretch of stalk, landing on his hands and knees between two oversized pebbles. "I think so," he murmured as he looked up at the very welcome sight of the worried faces of Cam and Spinach and Dilly.

"You'd better be!" Dilly snarled.

Nort blinked up at her. "Why?"

"Because I said so!"

"Oh. That's a good reason."

Dilly folded her arms. "Hmph. You can carry some of the vegetables."

Meg and Laddy decided to wait till nightfall so that it would be easier to sneak into the fortress. Meg smiled grimly to herself, picturing what Malison thought was taking place down here in her treasure cave.

While they were waiting, Laddy told Meg more about his journey, and then Meg told Laddy everything that had happened to her since she'd left her parents' castle. It took her quite a while to tell the story.

I've never seen a giant, Laddy told her. *Are you ready to go? It feels like night now.* He helped Meg down with one scaled claw and watched as she picked her way across the chamber. *Isn't it beautiful?*

Meg was trying not to twist her ankle on the glittering landscape, which kept sliding beneath her at unexpected moments. *Yes, Laddy, it's beautiful.*

At last she reached the other side, and Laddy showed her a small ladder made of metal rungs pounded into the stone. Meg climbed up. On this side there was no door, only a tunnel. Meg walked into the tunnel, glad for the occasional torch set into its walls. Laddy came along behind her, his breath warm on her back and his claws clicking faintly on the rocky floor. *Where does this go?* she asked.

To the mountainside above the fortress.

She lets you out? Meg had thought he was a prisoner.

She knows I won't stay away from my gold for very long, Laddy explained.

They were nearly to the end of the tunnel when something came flapping into the cave mouth. For a second Meg ducked, thinking it was bats, but then she realized that the magic scarf and the flying carpet had decided to show up again. They were both covered in sand, and one of the scarf's hems was torn out.

"Well!" Meg said, putting her hands on her hips. "You two should be ashamed of yourselves!"

The scarf and the carpet drooped in unison.

"You're off cavorting with seagulls and—and fish while I'm getting thrown into dungeons and Lex is quite possibly having his soul reconstructed in some sinister way by that *girl!*"

The scarf and the carpet turned to each other and shrugged, as if to say, We're here now.

Meg couldn't help smiling a little. "Come here." The scarf approached. "Did you get sand in your eyes, you flibbertigibbet?" The scarf closed its dozens of tiny eyelids as Meg brushed the sand off. "Your turn," Meg told the carpet, and Lex's magic conveyance flew over to her. "You'll have to hang sideways," Meg said. The rug tilted to hover on one edge, looking as if it were hanging from an invisible clothesline. Meg brushed and dusted the carpet vigorously on both sides. When she was done, a pile of sand lay in the middle of the rocky floor of the cave tunnel.

"That's better," Meg said. The scarf and the carpet gave themselves a couple of good shakes and hovered about expectantly. "Now, here's how you're going to help me get Lex back."

Lex sighed, putting down his book. It was a *very* good book, but Lex's tiny worry about Meg had stopped whispering and raised its voice gradually until it was simply shouting in his ear, refusing to let him concentrate on the magical uses of the hairs from a bechling's tail for another minute. Lex brightened. He couldn't do the kind of long-distance finding spell he'd done with Laddy's scale, but he didn't need to. Lex snapped his fingers, and three sparks appeared. "Go find Meg," he told them. The sparks twinkled, then split up, disappearing through three different walls with three faint fizzes. "Why didn't I think of that earlier?" Lex asked himself before he picked up his book and turned the page, having properly appeased the shouting worry.

He might have been surprised to know that Meg's scarf was doing exactly what he had sent his sparks to do, only the other way around, because Meg had told the scarf to search the fortress for Lex. However, unlike the sparks, the scarf couldn't fly through walls, so it was having a bit of trouble accomplishing its mission. Then it had the immense misfortune to fly into a great big room where a sorceress sat holding court. When she saw it, she jumped up. "What is that thing? Guards, catch it!" Whereupon the guards started leaping about the room, trying in vain to capture a scarf which simply flew higher, skimming along just beneath the ornate ceiling. Somebody threw a sword as if it were a spear. The man missed, but he gave Malison an idea. "Send for the archers!" she ordered.

The scarf shrilled angrily. All it wanted was to find the red-haired wizard boy, and instead strange people were throwing things at it. Pointy things, even.

The scarf dove, and one enterprising guard leaped, managing to catch it by one end. The others started to cheer, but their cheers changed to cries of astonishment and fear when the scarf twisted about in the guard's hands and struck, biting him hard on the cheek. The man let go and fell back, clutching his bloody face.

Free again, the scarf lunged upward, veered around a pillar, then dashed out the nearest doorway.

"After it!" Malison cried, and her guards streamed from the room like a nest of black ants after an intruder.

Young Nallis appeared in the doorway to the kitchen. "Something's happening!" she announced.

Stefka looked around, but most of the women didn't even bother to turn and listen. Alya had been turned to a statue, and that princess had been fed to a dragon. The servants had lost heart.

"What is it, girl?" Stefka wanted to know.

"I heard such a noise, and I peeped into the great hall, and they were all running around trying to catch a magic bird!"

"Magic bird?"

"Well, it looked more like a cloth to me, a scarf even,

but it was flying about like anything. They couldn't catch
it with their spears. So they've brought the archers, and
they're chasing the cloth through the halls!"

Luli put down her onion. "Magic scarves? What good
will that do anyone, I ask you? It's another of her tricks."

"Or the wizard boy's tricks. He was asking me about
his friend this afternoon," Nallis told them.

"Was he?" Stefka asked, interested. "What did you
say?"

Nallis blushed. "Nothing. I didn't know what to say."

"You were afraid of her finding out, weren't you?"
Stefka said kindly. She saw that the other women had
stopped their work to listen. Which was good, because
she had just been struck by a useful thought. "If the wizard boy knew what she'd done, maybe he'd help us."

"Get us turned to statues, more like," fat Imkuhl
said. "That Bain came around telling us we're slaves
now, not servants!"

"It's the same work as yesterday," Trena pointed out.

"She doesn't need to know we've talked to the boy,"
Stefka went on.

Imkuhl couldn't argue with that, but she wasn't finished, either. "The wizard is another one of hers, spell-
struck with dreadful loviness and sorceress-pleasing. Just
like my man Horth." Imkuhl sobbed only once before
she caught herself and forged ahead. "He may listen to
us, may lure us in with his devious magic ways. And then
he'll tell *her*—two seconds after he refuses to help us."

"Maybe, maybe not," Stefka said. "He's not in the dungeon, and he's not a statue like our Alya. He just sits in that workroom of hers, drinking hot chocolate and reading magic books." She appealed to everything her audience knew about people, which was quite a lot. "I don't think he'd be asking about the princess if he was under a spell." Several of the women nodded at this. Stefka clunked the pot she was carrying down on the nearest table for emphasis as she concluded, "We have to talk to him."

Malison gathered up her rustling night-black skirts and stalked through her fortress, trying to catch the attention of one of her guards long enough to find out where the creature had been seen last. They were clearly unable to catch it by their own efforts, and once again, she would have to provide her men with a magical solution. Magical—suddenly she stopped, scowling. Of course. The flying thing was probably some frivolous creation of that Lex boy. Malison turned to head for the library. *This time* she was going to show him exactly who she was: the Empress of the Southern Reaches, and soon of the Northern and Eastern and Western ones, too. No more hot chocolate and books for *him*! Malison was Empress of Absolutely Everything and Everyone There Was— including Lex.

21

Meg and Laddy flew around the fortress, peering in the windows of the second and third floors. Below them, Malison's guards made their rounds, never thinking to look up. Like the handful of guards on the roof, they had seen Laddy flying overhead before. Even if they saw him tonight, they wouldn't think much of it. At least, that's what Laddy had promised Meg. She hoped he was right, and that the guards wouldn't notice that their mistress's dragon was accompanied by a girl on a magic carpet.

It wasn't long before Meg and Laddy were treated to a glimpse of a horde of guards charging along a hall after something, arrows flying every which way. *Was that my scarf?* Meg asked, outraged. *That does it. I'm getting dizzy, and my scarf's in trouble. We're going in!*

All right, Laddy said calmly. He flew back to one of the larger windows. It wasn't exactly built with dragons in mind. *Don't hurt yourself,* Meg told Laddy as they neared the window.

I won't. Watch this! Meg backed off a little and hovered as Laddy circled away into the night, then came swooshing out of the darkness, shooting a bright stream of flame at the window. The glass melted, the metal rods holding the window together melted, everything melted and dripped down onto the surrounding stones. Just inside the window, Meg could see an ornate rug catch fire.

Guards began shouting above and below them as Laddy made another pass at the window, this time fanning hard with his wings. The rug inside burned brighter, but it soon died into a sad streak of black ash on the stone floor of the hallway. *Things should be cooler now,* Laddy said.

An arrow came flying up from below, nearly hitting the magic carpet and Meg. The magic carpet sailed in through the exact center of the now-empty window frame even as another arrow sliced the air where Meg's cheek had been a half second earlier.

As for Laddy, the dragon folded his wings tightly, rolled, and dove into the fortress on his back, a large red-and-gold arrow like the smaller rain of arrows that spattered harmlessly against his scaled back and sides as he went. Laddy slid monumentally down the hallway and hit a wall hard, crunching through it so that his head disappeared inside another room while the rest of him stuck out. His feet flopped about awkwardly.

Meg jumped off the magic carpet and ran to make sure her dragon wasn't hurt just as Laddy pulled his head free and gave it a good shake. *Laddy,* she began, when she heard an odd noise behind her. She turned around to see a young guard pointing and gasping, apparently unable to speak, he was so stunned by the sight of a dragon inside the fortress. At the very instant Meg realized she should stop the boy from telling someone where she was, another dark-clad figure came up behind him and shoved him hard through the doorway of the nearest room. The guard's attacker, one of the servant girls, quickly slammed the door, locked it, and pocketed the key. Then she turned to Meg. "I can see the dragon didn't eat you," she said cautiously, "but will it eat me?"

Meg smiled and spoke over the muffled cries and thumps of the guard trying to get out of his abrupt prison. "No, he won't. Can you help us find the wizard boy?"

The sparks slipped back into Malison's workroom and were beginning to tell Lex what they had learned when he heard a commotion out in the hall. "Just a minute." Lex went to the door, opened it, and stuck his head out, only to get plastered in the face by some kind of fast-moving flittery cloth object, after which somebody jumped through the door and pulled it shut behind them, nearly bashing Lex in the nose.

"What—" Lex pulled the cloth out of his eyes and was amazed to see that it was Meg's scarf, which seemed to be accompanied by three servant women. "What's the matter?"

Two of the women locked the door and leaned against it. The shouting in the hall got louder and somebody, or several somebodies, started pounding on the door. "Wizard," the third and oldest of the women said, "our mistress means to harm you. She has already done a horrible thing to your friend."

"You mean Meg? Where is she?" Lex looked around for his sparks. "My messengers told me she's in the sky, which makes no sense at all."

Stefka tried again. "The guards are here, and there will be trouble. But you must understand—"

"What. Happened. To Meg?" Lex interrupted. At that moment he seemed very wizardly indeed.

"The mistress threw her in the dungeon, and then she fed her—" the woman hesitated.

"She WHAT?"

Stefka rushed through the next bit. "I'm sorry to have to tell you this, but she fed her to the dragon. Since she was a princess, I mean. And now we need your help."

Lex looked as if he were about to bring the walls down, and indeed, the bookshelves trembled a little. Then a strange look came over his face. "Dragon, you say?"

"Dragon," Stefka repeated as the door started to shake. The other two women jumped away from it with twin yelps.

"There's something very important I need to know," Lex said. "What color is the dragon?"

But Stefka didn't get a chance to answer. The door burst open and a pack of guards tumbled in, baying for blood like so many hounds. They seized Stefka and the other two women before Bain stepped forward from among them to restore order. "What are you doing here?" Bain said curtly to the women, but he didn't wait for an answer. Instead he addressed Lex. "We're looking for a flying creature. A sort of dark blue, cloth-like being about this long." He showed the scarf's length with his hands just as the scarf peeked curiously over Lex's shoulder. Bain saw it, and his brows lowered. "Is the creature yours?"

"That's what I want to know," Malison said from behind Bain in the hallway. The guards parted to let her step into the room. "Is it yours?" she asked.

Something had changed, and it took Malison a second to realize what it was: for the first time since she'd met him, Lex didn't smile when he saw her. Instead he said, "I have a better question, and this time I want a true answer. What have you done with my friend Meg?"

Skinny Zlota burst into the kitchen, just as Nallis had done earlier.

"Now what?" Imkuhl grumbled.

"You know the poor little princess we were talking about?"

"Yes."

"She's back, and she's got that dragon with her—brought him right into the fortress!" Zlota lowered her voice. "I think she's going after the empress."

Imkuhl's eyes grew steely, and she looked around the kitchen. "Well, ladies, we'd better get up there and help her." She hefted her rolling pin. "Who's with me?"

"What have I done with that princess of yours?" Malison lifted her chin. "Whatever I wanted to do. *I* am the one who decides, you know."

"No, I don't know," Lex said hotly. "Where's Meg? And no more silly stuff about picnics, either. I've been hearing things about dungeons and dragons."

Malison gave the servant women a look, indicating that they would be held accountable for Lex's having been told something she didn't want him to hear. One of the women shrieked at the sight of the sorceress's eyes. "Take them away!" Malison ordered. The guards seemed almost as glad to leave the room as their prisoners did, shutting the heavy door hastily behind them.

Malison turned her gaze back to Lex. "Forget about your friend," she told him. "What matters now is that I'm tired of playing nice. I'm here to stop you, and it stops now."

"What?" Lex said, confused.

Malison sucked her breath in before she sneered, "Listen very carefully. I am an evil sorceress, and I am *not* going to let you get in the way of my magnificent plans, *Lex*." She said his name very sarcastically, as if it were a bad word—or worse, a stupid one. "Just because a few of the minor spells I've tried on you haven't had quite the intended effect doesn't mean I can't make things very, very bad for you." She really shouldn't have told him that, showing her weaknesses. Not that she had any. Flukes, maybe. Not actual weaknesses.

"You've been throwing spells at me?" Lex looked enlightened. "That explains the grogginess. And the headache. I even forgot about my sparks for a while."

"I turned you into a statue," the sorceress said proudly.

"My legs felt stiff," Lex said. "But I'm not a statue now." He sighed, clearly so disappointed in Malison that she almost felt a fleeting inclination to experience a minuscule twinge of actual guilt. "Is this going to be one of those wizard duels, then?" Lex asked in a quiet voice.

Malison hardened her heart again. She nodded hard, too, one quick dip of her chin.

"Fine." Lex flexed his fingers, ready because he had to be. For a moment, Malison didn't do much of anything. "Well?" he said. "What are you waiting for?"

All of the rage she'd been feeling ever since this boy set foot in her fortress burned through Malison. At her command, water poured down from the ceiling of the workroom as if it were a dark sky releasing the gates of the heavens. An avalanche of water from nowhere slammed down on Lex's head, drowning him—only it didn't. He just stood there, tilting one hand up, his mouth shaping a spell, and the water rode around him, seeking to hit the ground without hitting him.

Malison dropped her hands, and the water stopped falling. Enough of it had splashed around the room that she was a little wet herself, though her ordinary protection spells over the books had kept them dry. "Maybe we should do this in the throne room," she said sullenly, but Lex shook his head.

"Here is fine," he said, dismissing the water on the floor with a few words and a gesture. Then Lex snapped his fingers with both hands, calling out another spell.

Malison found herself surrounded by sparks that blinded her eyes. When the sparks faded, she saw that Lex was watching her with one bushy eyebrow raised quizzically.

The sorceress felt a surge of scorn. "Very pretty, but what does it do?" She sang a few words in an ancient language Lex couldn't possibly know. Demons began emerging through the floor, gnashing their blue teeth and reaching for Lex—but he said other words in the same language, and the demons disappeared.

Even worse, the infuriating boy seemed pleased and excited about what he'd done. Where was his *dignity*?

"Your turn," he said, almost as if they were playing a game.

Malison tried not to think of all the spells that had failed her. She just needed something bigger and better. She threw a mind-blanker at Lex, her spellwords ugly and spiky. He looked bewildered for a second, but his face quickly cleared, and he lobbed a torrent of goop at her, declaiming his own spell.

Malison ducked so that only her shoulder and one side of her hair turned pink. She didn't have time to wonder what else the spell was supposed to do. Malison slid a movement spell across the room, and for a few seconds Lex danced frantically, as if to an invisible fiddler.

She chanted.

He enchanted.

She hurled incantations—and accidentally hit the bookshelves. The books leaped from their shelves and started scuttling about the room, pages flapping.

Lex rebutted her incantations with alchemies.

The sorceress turned him into a salmon. He swiftly changed back.

He turned her into a dragonfly. She changed back, too.

She gave him old age. It faded away as he gave her infancy. With an effort, Malison babbled a spell to reclaim herself.

The words of their spells dove back and forth through the room, drawing magic after them like hooked fish pulling fishing lines through the water.

Malison focused again, trying a spell that wrapped the wizard boy in heavy chains.

Lex broke free and responded with a flock of chickens that flew at Malison, pecking her eagerly. Malison realized her arms were covered with kernels of corn. What kind of foolishness was this?

"Enough!" Malison roared. She spun around, flinging chickens and corn in every direction. Her anger grew larger than she ever thought it could, and she screamed her most terrible death spells at Lex.

His face calm, he answered her with a magic that rose on every side of the sorceress like a cylinder of glass, shimmering. None of her spells seemed to penetrate it, and when she put out her hands, they touched nothing, yet turned invisible where she should have seen them, sticking out into the workroom. Malison pulled her hands back hastily. She felt an unfamiliar twinge of fear as Lex moved toward her. But Bain was suddenly there, behind the wizard. He hit Lex on the head with a heavy bookend, and Lex fell to the ground. As he fell, his spell failed. The glassy cylinder was gone, and Malison was free.

Malison's eyes met Bain's. Had he realized she might have lost? Perhaps she should kill him before he could tell anyone else. No—for the moment at least, she wanted his help. "Very good, Chief Guard," she made herself say. And now she would kill the wizard.

22

RAGONS ARE LONG AND NARROW, ESPECIALLY when they fold their wings. It was a tight fit, but it worked, and Laddy flowed down the hallways of the fortress like water. Wherever he went, guards shouted and ran. When they got too close, Laddy spat fiery threats at them, and they kept their distance.

At first Meg was worried about someone coming up behind them. Her only rear guard was the magic carpet, and although it had been behaving itself ever since it got back from the beach, she was never quite sure when it would throw another tantrum and fly off in a huff.

Meg had only gone a little ways, however, when she saw that a dozen women servants had joined her, armed mightily with carving knives, rolling pins, and iron pots and pans. Every time Meg looked back, there seemed to be more women.

"Where are we going, exactly?" Meg asked Elva.

"To the mistress's workroom. That's where the wizard's been since you got here."

"Doing what?"

"Reading magic books, of course. She has a wondrous collection of magic books. My cousin Luli got to dust them once, and a big purple book bit her."

"I see." Meg rolled her eyes. All this time, while she'd been in peril of losing her life, Lex had been reading books. "I suppose he's been drinking hot chocolate, too?"

"Why yes, he has."

"I *see*," Meg said again. She had to remind herself not to bother being mad at Lex till later. First there was Malison to deal with. "I don't suppose Malison has some kind of perilous flaw we could exploit?"

Elva shook her head, then raised her voice over the noise of the fighting that had just sprung up behind them. Apparently some of the guards had attacked the servant women who were now acting as Meg's rear guard, and the women were giving as good as they got. Or giving better, considering how many guards were now lying on the floor as if they were sleeping on the job. Meg was reassured to see that the women were knocking the guards out rather than killing them. Still, Meg's little battalion managed to make up for their lack of deadly intent with the sheer force of their fury over the events of the past few weeks.

Lex's magic carpet helped out, too, coming up

behind guards and wrapping itself around them tightly so that the women could hit them, then spinning away to dump the guards on the floor here and there like heaped-up darkness.

To Meg's surprise, Elva wasn't a bit perturbed by the melee. She simply went on with her explanation. "When all of this first started, we were hoping she kept her heart inside an egg inside a bird inside a fish inside a cask at the bottom of a bottomless lake or some such. But she doesn't."

"That's a pity."

"Isn't it?"

They came around a corner and found themselves at the top of a broad stairway. Guards were pouring up the stairs toward Meg, while behind her the fighting had gotten fiercer. Battle cries rang through the air, or sometimes just recriminations.

"And to think I used to feed you supper every night, and a nice big breakfast every morning!"

"You always were a silly boy, Thomas Andrew Codriddle!"

"How dare you raise your hand to your own wife!"

"For the empress! Oof!"

As for Laddy, he sent the guards tumbling back down the stairs. But Meg's little party was advancing very slowly, and Meg was afraid they'd never get there. She longed for the feel of her sword in her hand, but Malison's guards had taken it away when they captured her.

Meg kept an eye out as they moved down the hall, till finally she discovered a sword. Meg guessed that the guard it belonged to was lying around somewhere with a big bump on his head, and she snatched up the sword with relief. It was longer and heavier than she was used to, but at least she was armed.

After three more turns, another stairway, and a lot of fire and shouting, Elva said, "Here we are. It's that door up there."

"Right there? Where the fifty guards are standing with their swords drawn?"

"That's the one!" Elva chirped.

Do you want me to burn them? Laddy said uncertainly. *Or should I just scare them a little?*

Malison had been so busy concentrating on her battle with Lex, she hadn't noticed what was going on outside her workroom. Into this new silence pounded the sounds of another battle, one raging in the hall. Malison paused. "What's happening?"

As if in answer to her question, Meg appeared in the doorway.

"You!" Malison cried.

"Me," said Meg. "And you'd better not have hurt Lex."

So exhausted from her duel she was practically swaying on her feet, Malison nevertheless managed to give Meg the benefit of her favorite wicked smile. "I could destroy you with only half a spell. Where's my dragon?"

"*My* dragon is in the hall, taking care of a few problems for me," Meg said coolly. She stepped into the room and moved quickly to stand beside Lex, who was sprawled near Malison's desk. Meg glanced down at her friend to make sure he was still breathing. She was madly relieved to see that he was. And here was her scarf, which had found Lex, just as she had asked it to. The scarf flew back to its usual place around Meg's neck and crouched there, blinking balefully at the sorceress.

"Next I suppose you'll tell me that's your cloth-creature," Malison said.

"As a matter of fact, it is." Meg's heart pounded, but she wasn't about to let Malison know that. She noticed that Malison's shoulder and part of her hair were pink. Did this girl actually outwizard Lex? No. "You must have cheated. You could never really have stopped Lex with magic."

Malison turned so red that Meg knew she was right. "I did not!" Malison said in exactly the tone someone would use if they had cheated. Behind her, Bain looked away politely, setting a bookend shaped like a bogwort down on the worktable.

"You hit him, didn't you?" Meg asked Bain.

Bain mumbled a non-reply.

"Come on, scarf," Meg whispered. The scarf made a brief sally toward Malison, but Malison spat a spell at it and the scarf fled, whimpering, beneath the worktable. Meg could only hope it wasn't hurt too badly.

"See what happens when you get in my way?" Mali-son demanded, seething. "I'll have to think of something more personal for you this time. Maybe you'd like to join the lizards under my throne. No, that's too easy, too *kind*." She sounded as if she were talking to herself now. "A merciful death is no good. Suffering is needed."

"Why?" Meg said. "I never did anything to you. But look what you've done to all these people!"

"It is my right and my nature," Malison informed her grandly.

"Excuses, excuses."

Malison drew herself up. "No more talk. I'm decid-ing your fate, you stupid girl."

"Again?" Meg thought fast. "Well, *I* have a spell from the enchanted forest. So it's your turn to tremble in fear, Mally."

"*Mally?*" the sorceress repeated in horror.

Meg pulled the shard of rose-painted china out of her pocket, wishing she had remembered it earlier, in the throne room. "Let everyone in this place go free— even him," she said, nodding in Bain's direction, "and I will spare you my wrath."

"Wrath? Puh-lease," Malison said. "Go ahead, serve me tea with that thing."

Meg waved the china around, wondering exactly how the spell was supposed to work. Finally she threw it at Malison's feet, where it shattered into several pieces. Malison laughed so hard she almost fell over.

The broken pieces of china quivered. There was a *poof*, and then the pieces were blank and white, as if they had never been painted. Meg looked up at Malison, who was now wearing a crown of red roses, real ones. Meg could even smell their perfume. "It's pretty," Meg said in bleak tones as Malison reached up to pull a rose out of her hair.

Malison tore the flower into little shreds. "Now then," she said briskly. "You were threatening me?"

Meg spared a harsh thought for Quorlock, although what she really wanted to do was slap Malison. She did have a sword, but swords weren't much good against sorceresses. Meg looked around for something magical to throw and noticed some knickknacks on the desk, in between the stacks of parchment. "What about this?" she said gamely, picking up a stone carved in the shape of an eyeball and hoping very much it was enchanted. "I think I'll threaten you with this eye-rock."

Malison stopped laughing. "Put that down. You could hurt yourself."

Meg selected another object with her free hand. It was only a wooden box, but it seemed to cling to her hand, and a dank whisper sounded in her head. "What about this one?"

"A priceless antique. Don't touch those artifacts, or you'll find yourself in worse trouble than even I could dream up for you."

Bain had been edging toward the door. "Excuse me, mistress. May I join the battle outside?"

"Go!" Malison snapped. She didn't need his help to deal with a mere princess.

Bain slipped out into the hallway, closing the door behind him.

Meg hefted the artifacts in her hands. She didn't have much choice at this point. While Malison was still looking away, Meg threw one artifact, then another. Malison yelped and managed to catch one in each hand, but before she could put them down somewhere safe, Meg threw a third artifact, and a fourth. The third one bounced off Malison before it let out a series of chiming notes and clattered across the floor. The fourth began leaking crimson smoke—but Meg was already flinging a fifth and a sixth at Malison, who cried, "Stop that!"

The fifth one released a swarm of bronze bees that immediately tried to sting the sorceress. Malison fought them off with a magic shield and then sent them away with a staccato wave of little pinging noises. Part of her hair had fallen out of its perfect arrangement atop her head, however, which pleased Meg inordinately. "Nyah, nyah!" Meg said, sticking out her tongue most undiplomatically and throwing two more artifacts.

Then she ran out of enchanted objects to throw, and Malison was still standing there. Well, her beautifully arched eyebrows had disappeared, but she looked perfectly capable of spell casting and more than insanely furious. Meg gulped. "Right, maybe a duel?"

"With *magic*?" Malison jeered.

Meg eyed the clunky sword she had dropped beside the desk and couldn't help picturing Malison turning her into a statue. "Of course." Magic, her worst subject. She sorted frantically through the spells in her head. She was probably the worst wizard in the land. The best wizard was unconscious, lying at her feet, and the second best was standing there in front of her, on the verge of magically torturing Meg till she died a miserable, bloody, or possibly transformed death.

"Keep it simple," she told herself. This was for Lex. And her parents. And the servant women. And even the guards.

But her mind had run out of spells to sort, and besides, everyone knew Meg's magic never worked the way it was supposed to. No wonder they had been so worried about her, she thought, flushing. She wouldn't have minded a little help from Gorba, or Dilly, or even Lieutenant Staunton at this moment. Meg had to be a hero *right now*. And there was nothing, nothing at all she could do.

"Poor goody-goody princess," Malison crooned.

Then suddenly Meg remembered a spell she had done once. It was supposed to foster learning and memory, but instead—well, Master Torskelly had been very unhappy. And Meg was out of time to think of anything better.

Malison smiled mockingly. "I just want to see one more of your ridiculous spells before you die," the sorceress said. "Waffles!" she added with a snort.

Meg searched in her heart for hope. Finding none, she fell back on sheer necessity. Meg cast her spell, saying the words softly one by one. "Josrif bakul dorsh." Had she even remembered it right?

At first nothing happened. Meg tensed herself to pick up the sword and defend Lex as best she could, for as long as she could, against Malison's power.

"That's it?" Malison said. "How *very* disappointing!"

Just then the sorceress sneezed. It was Meg's turn to smile. "What?" Malison said. And sneezed again.

And again.

And again.

And again.

Over and over, Malison sneezed, doubling over at the waist, she sneezed so hard. The sorceress waved her arms and tried to speak, but all she could do was sneeze and sneeze, and then sneeze some more.

Malison hadn't wanted a fair fight, and thanks to Meg, she had gotten her wish. Well, sort of, Meg thought. It's really very hard to cast a spell while sneezing, the princess of Greeve concluded happily.

23

NFORTUNATELY, BAIN REAPPEARED IN THE doorway, and he was frowning. "What have you done to the empress?" he asked.

In answer, Meg picked up her sword from where she'd dropped it and pointed it at Bain.

He didn't seem very worried. "Whatever it is, take it off."

Meg gave him an incredulous look. "So she can *kill* me? Um—no."

Bain advanced on her, brandishing his own sword. "You've caused a lot of trouble, Princess. That dragon of yours has my best men bottled up in one of the drawing rooms. And you appear to have corrupted the servants."

"Don't you mean slaves? Or should I call them your sisters and aunts and cousins?"

"Call them misguided," Bain said, sounding a lot like

Lieutenant Staunton. "Put down the sword before I'm forced to kill you."

"We can't have that," Meg told him, still half listening to the delightful sound of Malison sneezing. With blistering logic, she inquired, "How would Malison feel if you didn't save me for her to kill later?"

Bain paused. "Good point." He moved forward again with far too much grace and skill. "I'll simply have to disarm you. Perhaps maim you a bit."

Meg fended off his first blow. She knew very well this wouldn't last long. "Scarf!" she called. The scarf must not have recovered from Malison's spell. It whined once, but stayed where it had hidden itself.

"Laddy!" Meg yelled.

"He won't be able to hear you," Bain informed her, thrusting with near-deadly effect.

True, Meg thought. And she yelled again, this time in her mind. *Laddy!*

Meg managed to avoid Bain's blade for the second time, but when she attempted an offensive move, it didn't work in the slightest. She had to keep trying to block his attacks, and she wasn't very good at it. Master Zolis's advice about running away popped into her head. "Ha!" she said under her breath. She wished she had the option of fleeing Bain's onslaught, but she was utterly incapable of leaving Lex here on the floor, unconscious.

To think that Meg had wanted to see Bain again! She parried as best she could, panting. Then someone stepped into the doorway behind Bain, and she glanced up. Bain began to turn around, but it was too late—Stefka was already swinging her frying pan through the air. The pan met the guard captain's head with a satisfying CRACK!

Bain staggered. Stefka hit him a second time. This time Bain fell down and did not get up.

Meg felt a pang despite everything. "He's not dead, is he?"

Stefka checked Bain's pulse. "No. Just as well. Alya would have my head if he were."

In a sobering instant, they both remembered where Alya was. Stefka turned to look at Malison, who was still sneezing steadily, crouching over and straightening repeatedly, trying not to trip on the scampering books. "Well now, there's a sight," Stefka remarked.

The sounds in the hall had quieted, and Imkuhl stuck her head in the door. "Everything's under control out here. Oh!" she said, getting a look at Malison. Pretty soon half the women in the fortress were there, taking turns poking their heads into the workroom so that they, too, could enjoy the spectacle of Malison sneezing helplessly and crashing about.

"I don't know how long it will last," Meg said. "The only other time I did this, it went on for an hour or so."

Stefka knelt beside Lex. "If we wake him before the hour's up, will he be able to help us? Or did she vanquish him?"

Meg shook her head. "Bain hit him. I'm pretty sure he was winning."

"Or Bain wouldn't have hit him." Stefka turned her head to look at Bain, who was still lying on the floor. "Makes me even more glad I knocked him down."

"Fair's fair," Meg agreed. Then she thought of a question. "How did you know I needed help?"

"Your dragon swung his head about and nearly left us to go up the hall to you. I guessed what he was up to, so I told him I'd make sure you were all right."

On hearing this, Meg went to find Laddy and thank him for sending Stefka and for helping with the guards. He was sitting in the hall outside one of the parlors, intimidating the guards trapped within. *You're safe!* Laddy cried when he saw Meg.

Thanks to you. Stefka hit the guard captain on the head just in time.

Laddy surveyed his prisoners. *Did I do a good job?* he asked, although he already knew the answer.

You did a marvelous job, Meg told him. *I'm very proud of you!* Laddy lifted his head and posed heroically for her benefit. *You're the best dragon in the Southern Reaches,* Meg said, kissing him on his scaly nose.

What about the Eastern and Western and Northern ones?

Those, too, she assured him.

The next morning, Meg woke up in a nice, soft bed with a black satin comforter, happy not to be in a dungeon cell. After she had washed her face and put on a clean black dress, she went looking for Lex. She found him in a little parlor on the first floor eating a hearty breakfast of eggs and ham, served by half a dozen smiling women. Everyone was very pleased with Lex for unenchanting the guards and Alya and the lizards, not to mention putting a silence spell on Malison. The women served Meg, too, then left the two friends to their meal.

Meg was halfway through her second egg when it struck her. "Oh!" she cried. "Cam and Dilly and Nort and Spinach!"

"How many days do we have left? I've lost track," Lex confessed.

"So have I," Meg said, feeling guilty.

"You were a little busy trying to break out of the dungeon and not be eaten by a dragon," Lex reminded her.

"While you read books—"

"And drank hot chocolate. I know. I'm sorry, Meg. She clouded my mind a bit, but I shouldn't have believed her."

"You were right about her being beautiful," Meg said, testing the waters.

Lex blushed. "She is."

"She has a wonderful workroom, doesn't she?" Meg continued.

Lex leaned his chin on his hand and sighed wistfully. "She does."

"What's going to happen to the books?" Meg asked him.

Lex looked extra vague. "I, ah, thought I would send them back to my house in Crown."

"To keep them from falling into the wrong hands, of course," Meg said gravely.

"Some of them are very dangerous."

"Weren't those artifacts on her desk dangerous, too?"

"Oh yes," he said, and Meg had to smile. Then she wiped her mouth with a black napkin and got to the most important part.

"What about Malison and her fortress?"

"I can take the fortress down," Lex told her. "It's a very good spell, but it's still just a spell."

"And?"

Lex chewed for a while without answering.

"You're not thinking of giving her voice back, are you?" Meg persisted.

"Of course not."

"Well, in that case," Meg told him, "let her go. If she can't talk to spell-cast, she can't hurt anyone else."

Lex thought this over. "We shouldn't leave her in the village. They might get ideas about revenge."

"We'll give her a pack full of food and a few coins and send her on her way."

Lex agreed, to Meg's great relief. Then they tackled the problem of Lorgley Comprost. They decided it had been three days since they left the giant with his captives. "So we're meeting him day after tomorrow," Meg said. "Do you think we can find the thief by then?" She had recently realized that it wasn't enough for someone to be a powerful wizard: a magic-maker had to be able to figure out which spell to use in order to actually get something done.

"We have all those books," Lex said. "No, wait a minute! Malison has a scrying bowl. A really nice one."

"Why don't *you* have a scrying bowl?" Meg asked.

"I do, back at home," he informed her. "I just hardly ever use it."

"Because of your sparks?"

"Right. But they can't find a stranger without some idea of where to look. Scrying will be better."

"And then we can use the magic carpet to hunt him down and get the frobble back."

Lex looked dubious. "First let's find out where he is."

They left their hot chocolate cups behind, hurrying up the stairs to Malison's workroom to find the scrying bowl. It took Lex a little while to make the bowl cooperate. Meg read one of the now-quiet magic books while she waited.

"Ready," the wizard said at last. "Sit here so you can see, too."

Meg dragged a chair to the worktable and leaned over to watch Lex cast his thief-finding spell. After a moment, the water inside the silver bowl stirred and shifted, painting a picture. Then it stopped moving to hold the image clearly. "No!" Meg exclaimed in her astonishment.

The face in the scrying bowl was Bain's.

That night in the Sky Kingdom, the little group under the elm tree was unusually quiet. They had eaten dinner, but vegetables weren't particularly filling, so they were all hungry. Nort was as battered and bruised as if he had been in a fistfight. And then there was poor Crobbs. He had searched the elm tree for an hour before he had come down alone, thinking Nort had been eaten by a giant squirrel. After that, Crobbs had gotten lost trying to find the others to tell them the terrible news. The big blond boy was still in shock from the day's trauma. He seemed more upset than Nort over what had happened, sitting in a daze beside Cam.

Dilly rebraided Spinach's endlessly growing hair in the twilight while the others leaned against the tree trunk in silence. Finally Nort asked, "Crobbs, what did you see?"

"What?" Crobbs said, his voice dull.

"Today, up in the tree. When I looked, I saw the giants' house and part of the vegetable garden, then the well and a back wall. And a neighbor's house beyond that. What about you?"

Crobbs tried to think. "I saw leaves and branches."

"What else?" Nort asked patiently.

"I saw a wall, and a road, other houses. Rose bushes. And a well."

"The neighbors' well?" Nort asked.

Crobbs shook his head. "No. It's across the grass from this tree. Over in the corner in front of the house."

"Two wells?" Dilly said. "That's strange."

"Unless one of them is actually a doorway," Cam said.

"A *well*?" Nort asked dubiously.

"Could be. Maybe it doesn't look so much like a well up close."

"We could check," Dilly suggested.

"In the morning," said Nort. He clapped Crobbs on the back. "Good job!"

Crobbs smiled wanly.

There was no more talk of catching a bird.

The next morning, the five small people hiding out in Lorgley Comprost's yard split up again after a breakfast of slightly squishy vegetables. They had planned to go look at the well together, but Spinach's hair changed things. It had grown longer still and had gotten tangled up with grass and tree roots. The stuff wound around and around like a mad snake the color of straw. Dilly suspected that if they pulled it out in a straight line, the hair would reach clear to the front door of the giants' house. "Spinach," she said gently, "we really should cut it off."

Spinach clenched up her face and started to sob. "It's my hair!" she cried. "It's the only thing I have *left*! And you're just like that giant girl! She wanted to take it away from me, and now you want to take it away, too!"

Dilly stepped back, startled. It struck her that the things that had happened the last few days would be a bit much for anyone. They must have been especially trying for a girl who had been stuck in a tower for years—a girl whose greatest challenge in a very long time had been a whole lot of boredom. Her hair had been her only connection to the outside world, Dilly realized. No wonder Spinach was falling apart.

Nort and Crobbs seemed confused by Spinach's outburst, but Cam exchanged a meaningful look with Dilly over Spinach's head. Then he squatted next to Spinach, putting one hand on her shoulder. "You can keep your hair, Spinach. We'll just have to figure out a way to carry it."

"Right," Dilly said. "I'm sorry I said that. I'll help you get it sorted out so we can carry it more easily."

Spinach sniffled. "No cutting?"

"Not even a little," Dilly said reassuringly.

So it was decided: the three boys went off to examine the well while Dilly helped Spinach with her hair.

All of which was complicated by the fact that it was a beautiful day, and the giants had emerged from their house to weed the flowerbeds and hang the laundry out to dry. Dilly and Spinach spent the morning hiding in a hollow spot at the foot of the elm, pulling the hair in after them as best they could. It wasn't till lunchtime that they were able to come out and sit behind the elm's trunk to untangle Spinach's hair.

Nort and Cam and Crobbs were halfway across the grass to the well-that-might-not-be-a-well when the giants came out. They hit the ground and lay hidden, sure they were about to be discovered. Instead, they simply had a long, boring wait before they were able to scurry beneath the bushes and make their way from one bush to another, till finally they reached the well. It was late afternoon when they came back to the elm, just as Dilly finished rebraiding Spinach's hair.

"Well?" Dilly said.

Cam and Nort started to laugh, but Crobbs and Spinach looked confused. "*Well,*" Cam repeated. "That's where we went."

Dilly laughed a little, even though she didn't think it was that funny. "What did you find?"

"It's the door," Nort said soberly.

"That's wonderful!" Dilly exclaimed. "But if you found the door, why aren't you happy?"

"There's no ladder. No stairs," Nort explained.

"No way down?" Spinach asked. "Then how does the giant do it? Can he fly? Is he magic?"

Nort and Cam shrugged while Crobbs stared at the ground.

"Lex and Meg might be back soon," Cam told the others, trying to raise their spirits.

"Maybe we should have stayed in that dollhouse," Nort said.

Spinach turned pale.

"No," Dilly said firmly. "It's better to be free."

Even so, they passed a very hungry and dispirited night beneath the elm tree.

Only to wake up and find that Spinach's hair had taken over the world.

time
do

24

BAIN KNOCKED ON THE DOOR OF THE WORK-room lightly before he stepped in to face Lex and Meg, looking sheepish. "I brought your sword back," he told Meg, holding it out.

He'd been the one who had given it to her in the first place. Then he had taken it away as Malison's henchman, and now he was giving the silver-hilted sword back again. It was really very odd, Meg thought as she stood to belt the sword around her waist. "Thank you," she said without smiling. She'd been avoiding Bain ever since Lex took Malison's spell off the night before.

"I'm the one who has to say thank you," Bain said. "Thank you for saving me. For saving all of us."

Meg snorted softly. Bain was back to his usual charming self, but he'd caused ten kinds of trouble while he was enchanted.

"There's something else," Lex said.

Bain threw up his hands. "I wish I didn't remember everything I did while I was under that spell, but I do." He addressed Lex humbly. "I'm sorry for a lot of things, but first, I want to apologize for hitting you on the head last night."

"Right when I was corralling Malison," Lex said.

"Right then. I was just—"

"Doing your job," Meg said.

"And I'm sorry about the sword fight," Bain told her. "Good thing—well, it's just a good thing." He felt the side of his head. "I've still got the bump to show for that."

Meg finally smiled. "Thanks to Stefka."

"I've got one, too," Lex said stiffly.

"Sorry again," Bain told the wizard. "Anyway, everything's going well now." He looked more closely at their faces. "Isn't it? What's wrong?"

"It's about something you stole," Meg said.

"Not anymore. I'm a reformed bandit, remember?"

"Something you stole from a *giant*?" Lex said meaningfully.

Bain was speechless. When he had recovered his voice, he sputtered, "It's not—well, I—*how do you know about that*?"

Lex tapped the scrying bowl. "I have my sources."

"And because you stole from that giant," Meg went

on, trying to speak calmly, "Dilly and Cam and Nort and one of my father's guardsmen are now the giant's prisoners. His *hostages*."

Bain grabbed a chair and sat down. *"Really?"*

"Really."

"I suppose he wants it back," Bain said. "Though I don't have it anymore."

"Where is it?" Meg asked.

"Why don't you talk to your dragon friend?" Bain said ruefully. "Malison took everything we had and set him to guarding it."

"That's not all," Lex told Bain. "The giant doesn't just want his treasure back. He wants you, too."

Bain moved forward to the edge of his chair as if he were thinking of making a run for it, but then he sank back down. "I suppose you want me to pay for my crimes."

"We want you to help," Meg said.

Bain gave her a bittersweet grin. "For you? I'll help."

When Dilly woke up, there was hair everywhere. She coughed and sat up. Her face was full of hair. Around her, the others were struggling to pull free of Spinach's hair, which had come loose from its braid during the night and was piled so high that they had to swim their way through it, frantically searching for a way out.

At last they emerged and sat to one side of the hair, panting. "This is absurd," Nort said.

Spinach started to cry again. Clutching two handfuls of hair to her face to wipe her eyes, she wailed, "You can't make me cut it!"

"Why does it keep growing like that?" Cam said, baffled.

Dilly looked at him for a long moment and then jumped up. "Spinach!" she said excitedly. "Has your hair ever grown this long before?"

Still crying, Spinach shook her head. "No. Never. It was just the right length for my tower."

"Aha!" Dilly said triumphantly. The others stared at her in confusion, so she sat back down to explain. "Don't you see?" She grabbed up two handfuls of hair herself. "This hair is our way down!"

"What?" Crobbs said. "Hair?"

Spinach's eyes grew wide and she let out an even louder wail, so loud Cam thought maybe the giants could hear it inside their house. "You're just saying that so you can cut it off!" she sobbed.

"No, listen," Dilly said. "Cam got it right. *Why* is the hair growing so long? So very, very long?"

Spinach's crying subsided. "Why?" she asked, sniffling. "I don't even know, and it's my hair."

"Because it's *helpful* hair," Dilly said. "It's hair that's meant to reach from a high point like your tower"—she held one hand high—"to a low point." She put the other hand low.

"To the ground," Cam said, enlightened.

"Hair?" Nort said. "We're probably miles up in the sky, in a magic sky land. There's no way hair could take us clear to the ground."

"Magic sky, magic hair," Dilly said tartly.

"It's *helpful* hair," Spinach told Nort, her lower lip stuck out defiantly.

"Very helpful," Cam said thoughtfully. "And we really will have to cut it off."

Spinach opened her mouth to cry again, but Cam said hurriedly, "Only so we can get you down, too."

"It will grow back," Dilly reminded Spinach. "It grew back after Loris cut it."

"That's true." Spinach seemed a little calmer now. "It grows back very fast."

Nobody could argue with that. They felt like they were sitting in the middle of a hayfield, there between the elm tree and the stone wall.

"It *can't* be long enough," Nort repeated.

"If we dangle her down the well—" Crobbs began, but Cam shot him a look, and he stopped.

"We could go and camp by the sky-well tonight to sort of encourage your hair, and then we'll give it a try tomorrow morning after it's grown even longer," Cam said. "I'll go first."

Dilly noticed that everyone was nicer to the hair once they had decided it wasn't out to choke them, that it maybe even meant to help them. The other four worked to untangle Spinach's hair and laid it out in a long, long line, till they got so far they had to double back. And double back again. And again. "I'm afraid to braid it," Dilly said. "Then when it grows, the whole thing's a mess."

"Just for the trip to the sky-well," Cam suggested, so that's what they did. In the end, they each looped great coils of braid over their shoulders and suspended more hair between them. When everyone was in place, they embarked on the trek through the grass to the well-that-wasn't-a-well.

"Hair," Crobbs was heard to mutter incredulously every so often, and even Dilly was tempted to agree with him. Besides which, she thought, everyone was still a little jumpy about Nort's most recent adventure. Fortunately, they were able to get to their new campsite, a thick bush that grew near the well, without any further trouble. Cam, Dilly, and Crobbs set off on another journey to the garden to find food, while Nort and Spinach stayed beneath the bush with the very helpful hair, neither admitting to the other that they were watching the sky for crows.

After the villagers went back to their homes, Laddy was the only permanent resident of Malison's fortress. Well, Laddy and Malison. Now Laddy was worried. *I know the treasure is all mine, but everyone else knows, too. Those guards know. And that Bandit Queen,* he told Meg as they sat together on the floor of the empty throne room.

Meg leaned against Laddy's warm side, figuring out something she really didn't want to figure out. For days, she'd been wanting to find Laddy and bring him home with her—but she had to admit to herself that going back to Hookhorn Farm wasn't what he needed. With an inner wrench, Meg made herself do the right thing.

What I think, Meg told Laddy, *is that there are other caves in these mountains.*

I guess so.

You could scout around and find a much better dragon lair, one nobody knows about.

Not even you? Laddy sounded surprised.

Meg resisted the impulse to tell him what to do. *You can show me if you want, but you don't have to.*

Laddy looked around his current home. *This isn't so bad.*

But it's not truly yours. It's still Malison's place. You need to find a place that's just yours—so no one will know where it is except the mountain goats.

Mountain goats?

I've heard they taste almost as good as sausages, Meg informed him.

But not as good as princesses, Laddy said slyly.

Very funny. Go on now. Find a lair.

I will, Laddy said, *a really good one!* He was already starting to sound like a proud homeowner.

Soon afterward, Laddy went off on his house-hunting expedition. He was gone for hours, and Meg tried to keep busy. A fire-breathing dragon isn't likely to run into anything he can't handle, she told herself.

At twilight, Laddy came back to tell Meg that he had found a marvelous lair. *I sniffed the way I sniffed for treasure, but this time I sniffed for lairs,* he explained, which Meg took to mean he had used his dragon magic. *It has rocks, and long tunnels, and a nice high ceiling deep inside!* he told her excitedly.

Meg still felt funny about all this, but she congratulated Laddy just the same.

Soon Laddy was hauling gold and jewels through the darkening skies, flying silently from the far side of the fortress into the mountain wilds. Meg decided he looked like an owl with a strange, gleaming mouse in its claws. Back and forth he went for most of the night, until finally he had taken everything to his new home except the giant's frobble, which he gave to Meg with some reluctance early in the morning.

His real reason for waking Meg up well before sunrise was that he had decided he *did* want to show her his new lair. Very pleased, a yawning Meg borrowed Lex's carpet without asking. She and Laddy flew over the nearest mountain, then swooped in and out of a series of narrow gorges to reach the cave.

Laddy's lair was much prettier than Malison's treasure chamber had been. It was easy for Meg to praise the cool, dark tunnels, the stalactites and stalagmites, and the underground stream with its gleaming marble bed.

Laddy was so proud he nearly melted a pile of gold hel-
mets as he rushed around pointing out all of the best
features of his new home to Meg. They were both smiling when they flew back to the fortress. Meg kept smiling
as she and Laddy said their goodbyes. *I'll come see you soon,*
Laddy told her.

I can't wait, Meg said.

Once he was out of sight, she sniffled a little. But
only a little.

There was one more goodbye before Meg and Lex went
to meet the giant with Bain. Alya had invited them to a
farewell breakfast in the fishing village, which turned out
to be named Herring. Ugly, but apt, Meg thought. As
they walked down the road, she noticed happily that the
flowers in everyone's window boxes were being watered
again. A few were even blooming.

Alya's house was painted green, with a blue door. Lex
sniffed as they knocked. "Whatever that is, it smells deli-
cious."

Inside, the house was tidy and friendly, the only
incongruous note an array of swords proudly displayed
on the wall along with some embroidered scenes in
frames.

Embroidery. Ugh. "Did you embroider those?" Meg
made herself ask.

"No," the former Bandit Queen said. "But the
swords are mine."

"What do you do now?" Lex said as they sat down to eat.

"She's a baker," Bain told them. "At first everything she made came out like rocks."

"Not anymore." Alya slashed a look at her brother.

"Not anymore," Bain said. "And one of the fishermen's been coming around giving her gifts of haddock and mussels."

"So I make soup out of them," Alya said. She changed the subject. "Go on, Bain, tell them what you do."

"I hunt," he said. "It's what I know."

"That and chief guarding," Meg murmured. Bain studiously ignored her.

Alya's baking didn't taste anything like rocks. Meg had two slices of peach crumble, and Lex had three.

"What was it like to be a statue?" Meg asked Alya. "Could you hear anything? Feel anything?"

Alya grimaced. "Oh yes. That horrible voice yelling for strawberries, for maps, for prisoners." She glanced at her brother. "And my own brother answering, 'Yes, mistress. Whatever you say, mistress.' " She said this last bit in a deep, lovesick voice, and Bain had the grace to flush.

"That's all I ever heard him say," Meg agreed.

"So you didn't get to hear him talk about Malison's beauty?" Alya asked.

"Alya!" Bain nearly turned purple.

His sister grinned. "I guess not."

25

THE FIVE HUMANS BENEATH THE BUSH WERE slumbering so soundly that they didn't even wake up when Lorgley Comprost came out of his house the next morning and climbed into the doorway to the Belowlands. *Anyone* would sleep well if they were not only exhausted, but were pillowed on a mattress of enchanted hair.

Before they had gone to bed, Dilly, Cam, Nort, and Crobbs had arranged the hair carefully into a wide pillow, leaving room for it to grow over to one side, next to Spinach's head.

Now only Cam stirred, and by the time he tore himself out of sleep and stumbled over to look, first having to climb the stones to the top of the well, Lorgley's stairway had already faded from sight. Cam could see nothing but blue sky down the well. He told himself he must have imagined hearing something and went back to where the others were still snoring. "Just a little longer," Cam said before he yawned and dropped off again.

"You're sure he'll be here?" Meg said. She and Lex and Bain were waiting in the meadow at the edge of the enchanted forest, right where they had last spoken to the giant.

"He promised," Lex said. "He's probably finishing his breakfast."

"What do you think he'll do?" Bain seemed awfully tense. "I mean, I don't usually come back to the scene of a crime like this."

"You have the frobble. That will help," Meg said, trying to be encouraging.

Lex glanced up. "Look."

They could see Lorgley's feet first, then his long legs, marching down the sky stairs that hadn't been there a moment before and that weren't there again as soon as Lorgley touched the ground.

"Giants have magic?" Meg asked.

"Family spell," Lex explained, and Meg wondered how he knew. But Lex was busy riding the magic carpet up to talk to Lorgley, so she didn't have time to ask. The wizard and the giant conferred. Meg and Bain couldn't hear Lex's voice from the ground, while Lorgley's voice was an unintelligible rumble.

As the giant crouched to greet them, Meg waved. Lorgley waved back, his huge mouth quirking into a smile. The giant didn't smile at Bain, though. He took a closer look and said. "YES. THIS IS THE THIEF."

Bain bowed, holding up the frobble, which was sort of a blob-shaped gold vase. It was so small by giant standards that Meg suspected humans must have made it. Now Lorgley put out his huge hand, and Bain climbed over the giant's fingertips to lay the frobble across it. He climbed back down rather hastily.

Meg couldn't keep from interrupting. "But what does it *do*?" she shouted.

"WATCH." The giant touched the blobby vase in the center of his palm. The frobble shimmered, and suddenly a small pond lay in Lorgley's hand. Lilies grew on either side, while golden frogs leaped across it. A fish with emerald eyes lifted its head out of the water. The reeds beside the little pond played a melody that made Meg want to climb onto the giant's hand and listen forever.

Lorgley touched one of the reeds with the tip of a great finger, and the frobble changed back into an ugly vase, sitting solidly in his hand. "MY LITTLE DAUGHTER LIKES IT," he explained.

"Do *you* like it?" Bain asked Meg softly.

"Of course," she whispered. "It was beautiful. You didn't know it did that?"

"I had heard. I couldn't figure out how to make it happen, though. Nothing I tried worked."

"WELL, THIEF? WHAT DO YOU HAVE TO SAY FOR YOURSELF?"

"I'm very sorry," Bain yelled. "It's just that I wanted a wonderful gift for my ladylove."

Meg stiffened. So there *was* a bandit girl.

Lorgley smiled slowly. "IT *IS* WONDERFUL."

This was all very nice, but where were the hostages? In his hat? In his pocket? "Sir," Meg called, "Where are our friends?"

Now it was Lorgley's turn to look ashamed. "I'M AFRAID THEY ESCAPED."

"You lost them?" Meg hollered. "What are we supposed to do?"

"I DON'T KNOW. IF THEY COME BACK, I WILL BRING THEM DOWN TO YOU. I THOUGHT THEY WERE HIDING IN THE FLOWERBEDS, BUT WE SEARCHED AND COULD NOT FIND THEM."

"That's not fair!" Meg exclaimed. "We brought you the frobble *and* the thief!"

"NO," Lorgley said, "IT ISN'T FAIR. WHICH IS WHY I WILL LET YOU KEEP THE THIEF."

Bain looked hopeful.

"Meg," Lex said. "We'll find them. He really doesn't know what to do about it."

"I suppose not." It wasn't as if they were keeping Bain

in exchange for the others. She and Lex would find Dilly and Cam and their two companions, and everyone would be together again. Bain could go home—to his "ladylove," she thought with an inner sniff. The rest of them could go back to her parents' castle where they belonged. After all, Laddy was fine now. Once Meg had found the rest of her friends, everything would be just perfect and her quest would be over, a job well done. So Meg told herself crankily as she got ready to say goodbye to Lorgley Comprost.

They were about to shake hands with the giant, or touch fingertips or something, when Meg and Lex and Bain heard an odd popping sound, and Malison stood before them, lifting her hands triumphantly and sneering around in a way that was probably meant to be sinister, but instead just seemed smug.

"Not *again!*" Meg cried. She felt her scarf slip behind her back to hide.

The giant looked down at the newcomer, puzzled.

Malison spun about, pointing at each of them in turn. "I will feed *you* to the swamp monsters of Slirlin," she told Meg. "And *you* will carry the stones to build my new fortress one at a time, with your teeth," she told Bain. "As for you," she said to Lex, "*you* I will shrink to the size of an ant and keep in a jar on my desk! Right next to the Angled Orb of Non-being, as soon as I get it back, you thief!"

"I THOUGHT *HE* WAS THE THIEF," Lorgley said,

indicating Bain, but Malison ignored the giant, which was pretty hard to do, considering his size.

"*Now* do you believe me?" Meg demanded, glaring at Lex.

"I just—"

"You just made it temporary, didn't you?"

Lex hung his head. "I was hoping maybe she'd learned her lesson."

"Lesson?" Malison said scornfully, determined to have everyone's attention. She threw a spell in Bain's direction, and he stood up a little straighter. "Mistress, how may I serve you?" Bain said in somber tones.

"Oh no," Meg grumbled. "The guard captain's back."

Malison began a complicated spell, but she paused to order Bain, "Don't just stand there! Hit the wizard!"

Lex shook his head. "That only works when I'm not expecting it." He pointed his left pinky finger at Bain and said a single piping word. In the space of a heart-beat, Bain turned into a brown puppy. He barked and ran to Malison's side, begging her to play.

"There *is* such a thing as too much black," Lex told Malison.

She shoved magic at him with a bloodcurdling yell, but nothing happened.

"It's not like I haven't changed my protection spells since last time I saw you," Lex said.

Malison threw spell after spell at Lex as Bain frol-icked around her feet and Lorgley and Meg watched in amazement. The sorceress was making herself hoarse, but nothing worked, not even a little. "NO!" Malison screeched, and she kicked the puppy.

"Lex," Meg growled, not even noticing that Malison had just decided she would be better off casting spells on Meg.

"Got it," he said, as angry as Meg had ever seen him. Lex usually hemmed and hawed over picking just the right spell, but now he suddenly towered, his vivid hair standing up like forks of lightning and his normally kind eyes turning hard. Even as the words of Malison's next spell leaped from her mouth, Lex's incantation took hold of the sorceress. The ground shook and Meg lost her footing, falling down in a heap.

When she sat up, a very beautiful life-size doll with long black hair lay on the grass in front of her.

Lex, who was starting to look like his usual self again, turned to speak to Lorgley. "A gift for your daughter."

"I SEE," Lorgley said gruffly. He tucked the frobble in his shirt pocket and reached for the doll. "THERE'S NO CHANCE—"

"None," Lex assured him.

"I SUPPOSE HER MOTHER DOESN'T NEED TO KNOW WHERE I GOT IT."

"Just what I was thinking," Lex said.

"WELL THEN. GOOD DAY." The giant picked up his hat and turned to go, carrying the sorceress doll very carefully. Out of nowhere, a stairway glittered into existence. Lorgley Comprost walked heavily up it into the clouds. Soon all they could see were the giant's feet, and then nothing, until the stairway itself shivered to match the sky and then disappeared altogether.

Lex stood staring after the giant, his smile slowly shifting into an uneasy expression.

"Are you going to change Bain back?" Meg asked him. She had to say it twice before Lex heard her. Lex called the puppy to him and whispered in its ear. Instantly, the puppy changed its shape and became Bain. "What happened?" he said, confused.

"Lex turned you into a puppy and Malison into a doll," Meg told him.

"Why?"

Meg couldn't help rolling her eyes. "She enchanted you again."

Bain groaned. "Not 'Yes, mistress.' "

"I'm afraid so," Meg said. "We gave the doll to the giant for his daughter to play with."

Lex said nothing. He just stood there looking troubled. Meg patted his arm. "I know it was hard, but you did the right thing, Lex. Truly."

"She didn't give you much choice, did she?" Bain said.

Lex acted like he hadn't heard either of them. "Why don't people believe me when I tell them I'm the greatest wizard in the known kingdoms?" he asked plaintively.

"Well, except for that very old wizard on the Isle of Skape."

"I heard he died," Bain said, trying to be helpful.

"Oh." Lex gulped. Apparently he had liked knowing about the elderly wizard. "So I really am? The best, I mean?"

"Yes," Bain explained. "Only I think you'll find that most of the time it's the people who aren't actually the best who go around saying that they are."

"So they're lying, these people." Lex was thoroughly perplexed.

"They're bragging," Bain said, giving Meg a swift look.

"Lex," Meg said. "*I* know you're the best, and *Bain* knows you're the best, and that's enough."

"It is?"

"You *are* the greatest wizard for miles around," Bain said. "But . . ." He looked at Meg again.

"But," Meg said, "that's not very important."

Lex drew himself up, looking more suited to his status than he usually did. "Malison thought it was," he said, offended.

"Malison's a doll!" Meg exclaimed. "She didn't understand that being a wizard isn't nearly as important as, as . . ." She paused.

"As hot chocolate?" Lex ventured.

"Exactly!" Bain exclaimed. "Not to mention having the kind of friend who would take on a sorceress to protect you because you've been knocked on the head, never mind by whom."

"With a sneeze spell," Lex said, chuckling. "She stopped that girl with a sneeze spell."

"All right, already," Meg griped, secretly feeling relieved. She suspected that somehow a disaster of far greater than Malisonian proportions had just been averted, and from the look in Bain's eyes, he felt precisely the same way.

ti

26

THE SUN ROSE HIGH, BUT STILL THE FIVE travelers slept behind the flowering bush, Cam having gone back to sleep with the others. When they finally woke up, it was to the sight of the giant emerging from the sky-well. "We could have gone with him," Dilly cried.

"Shh," Nort told her. "He would have taken us back to that dollhouse. Besides, we have Spinach's hair."

"Get ready," Nort said as Lorgley went in his front door and shut it behind him. "Now it's our turn." He found himself looking around for the two enchanted squirrels, but there seemed to be no way of catching up with them. He hoped they would be safe.

"I'm first, remember?" Cam said.

"Right." Nort looked at Dilly. "What are we going to do with you?"

"Me?"

"You're afraid of heights," Spinach said in cheerful tones. She'd been far too happy ever since her hair had become the hero of this little endeavor, Dilly thought sourly.

"I hadn't forgotten," Dilly told the others.

"Why are you afraid?" Spinach asked. "Is it because you're usually down low? Is it because—"

"This is a lot higher, is the problem," Nort explained before Spinach could ask any more questions.

"You're not helping, saying that," Dilly hissed.

"I'll bring her down again," Crobbs said.

There didn't seem to be a better solution.

They had unbraided Spinach's hair the night before, trusting it to grow longer before morning. Now they laid it out in a series of long lines, looping back and forth in the shadow of the sky-well, away from prying eyes in the giants' house. Dilly started at the back of Spinach's neck and braided till her hands cramped, then Nort took a turn, and then Cam, and finally Crobbs. Then they all took another turn, and another, until finally they had a fantastically long rope made from Spinach's hair.

"Are you ready?" Cam asked Spinach.

She looked a little anxious, but she nodded. Cam took his knife out and with great care used it to cut Spinach's braid off just above her shoulders. "Thank you."

Spinach lifted her chin. "You're welcome."

It took some doing to secure the rope in the sky-well, but they found a huge metal hook that must have held a bucket long ago and double-looped the braid around that. Cam climbed gingerly into the well's gaping mouth. "If you feel the braid go loose, then wait a minute. It will mean I've reached the bottom, and after that I'll give the braid three short tugs. Which will mean it's safe for the next person to come down."

"And if the braid's not long enough?" Spinach asked.

"Then I'll climb back up."

"What if your weight disappears, and we don't feel any tugs?" Spinach persisted.

"Spinach!" Dilly said sharply.

Cam looked around at the others. "That will mean something else, won't it?" With those words, he grasped the rope of hair and began his descent.

Meg and Bain and Lex climbed back onto the magic carpet, arguing about the best way to find their missing friends. "We should have gone with Lorgley," Meg said. "They're somewhere up there—they have to be!"

"That's why we have a magic carpet," Lex told her. "A very *nice* carpet," he said as the carpet gave a little lurch.

"Yes, but how will we find the Sky Kingdom? You think it's just sitting up there on top of the clouds?"

"It was when I went," Bain said.

"How *did* you get up there?" Lex asked.

Bain grinned. "I waited for the giant to come down and hitched a ride."

"He didn't notice?" Meg said.

"He was bringing back some timber. I hid in the bundle."

And that's when all this trouble started, Meg thought but did not say. She tried to pinpoint the exact spot where Lorgley had disappeared. "We should go straight up where those stairs were and look around."

"Carpet, follow that giant!" Lex said. "The one who just left."

The magic carpet rose slowly into the air. They were well above the tree line now, up toward the clouds, but they couldn't see anything. Just mist.

They flew still higher, then searched and searched, looping aimlessly about in the area where they had last seen Lorgley. Finally they went back down to eat the lunch the village women had packed for them. After that they flew back up to try again.

"Meg, we may never find them," Lex said.

"Keep looking!" she said with gritted teeth. "Bain, how did you get back down?"

He made a face. "It wasn't easy. There was this bird . . . Anyway, it won't help us now."

"I'm thinking pretty soon they'll get hungry and talk to Lorgley," Lex said. "Then he'll bring them back down for us."

"No," Meg said in a strange voice, "he won't."

"Why not?" Lex asked.

"Because Cam's right over there." She pointed at the nearest cloud, off to their left.

Lex thought she was imagining things, but he didn't want to argue with Meg in her current mood, so he asked the carpet to go over to the left. Suddenly they were hovering in the air directly in front of Cam, who nearly lost his grip on the rope he was clinging to when he saw them. "Meg?" Cam managed to say. "You came back!"

"Of course I did," she said, with a knowing smirk for Lex and Bain. "Let's get you down."

It took a while, but after various trips up and down on the magic carpet, Dilly's with her hands covering her eyes, the five travelers from the giants' house were safely back on the ground below. Lex had gone up the sky-well again, this time to let Lorgley Comprost know what had happened.

"You mean, he would have brought us down?" Crobbs said, bewildered. "Nort didn't have to get batted around with a broom or half eaten by a crow?"

"Yes, he did," Dilly said firmly. "Spinach and I could not have stayed in that dollhouse one minute longer."

"True," said Nort, with a glance at Dilly. "Me neither." Nort was talking with his mouth full, but nobody seemed to care. Meg and Bain had prepared a second picnic for the hungry new arrivals, who were happily eating everything they could get their hands on.

"What about you?" Cam asked Meg. "Did you have any adventures? How did you find the thief?"

"A few things happened," Meg said. "Have another meat pie for now. I'll tell you about it later."

Cam was glad to oblige. He and Dilly and Crobbs acted as if they were starving. "I never want to see another vegetable in my life," Dilly moaned.

"I do," said Spinach.

"Really?" Cam looked at her.

"I've decided vegetables are nice."

Dilly inspected Spinach's hair. "It's down to your waist again."

The braid rope hadn't reached the ground. Cam had insisted on checking. It stopped about thirty feet up, though, which Nort said was pretty close.

"Besides," Dilly said loyally, "we didn't give it a chance to finish growing. It would have reached the ground if it had had time to grow a little more. Right, Rosalina Liliana?"

"Right, Cookie Ann."

While the others were still eating and talking, Bain motioned to Meg. She followed him reluctantly along the edge of the forest till they came to a spot where a fallen tree cut across the field. "Have a seat," Bain said, gesturing to the log.

Meg sat, but she refused to smile.

"What's wrong?" Bain asked. "You have your friends

back, and Malison is gone for good. Aren't you happy?"

"I'm fine," she said tightly. "Just like you're fine. You and your ladylove," she added, though she immediately wished she hadn't.

"I wanted to do something grand for her," Bain said, looking thoughtful. "Something that would make her smile at me, not to mention something that would make a king sit up and take notice."

"A king?"

"Meg, I stole the frobble for *you*."

"What?"

He said it again.

Meg gaped. "You robbed a giant—for me?"

"Yes," Bain said, seeming uncharacteristically awkward.

"That's so—well, I can't say it's sweet, exactly, but it's"—Meg scrambled for a word—"impressive."

"It is, isn't it?" Bain said, his confidence quickly restored.

"You're saying you like me?"

Bain nodded.

Meg had never imagined, not really. She just couldn't. A picture of Bain looking adoringly into Malison's eyes popped into her mind. "I don't believe you," she snapped.

"Why not?" Bain was genuinely surprised.

"Because the day before yesterday, no, this very afternoon, you were gawping at an evil sorceress as if she were the most wonderful thing ever!"

"I was under a *spell*," Bain protested. "I was a puppy last time it happened!" He had to grin. "Puppies look at everyone that way."

"I suppose." Meg scowled, kicking the dirt. "I don't notice things like Dilly does. I don't think I'm very good at it. This romance stuff, I mean."

"Who is?" Bain replied.

Meg brightened. "Really?"

Bain, who usually seemed a bit too clever for his own good, shook his head. "Nobody's any good at it."

"But those flowers and the minstrel songs that rhyme 'dove' and 'love' with 'heaven above'—"

"They're pretending," he explained. "Everybody pretends, and sometimes it turns out all right."

"Huh. So—there's no bandit girl?"

"Nope." Bain tossed his dagger high into the air and managed to catch it again without stabbing either himself or Meg. "Ever since last year, I've been thinking about you. Alya told me I was crazy."

"Well, you are, a little."

"Ha."

Meg thought of something. "It's not just because I'm a princess, is it?"

Bain caught her hand and pulled her to her feet. "Princesses are a lot of trouble." He twirled her in a circle. Completely forgetting Master Deedle's dancing lessons, she stepped on his toes. "But princesses who get through enchanted forests in one piece and defeat evil sorceresses without involving any armies and rescue their lost friends from the sky are worth the trouble."

He let go of her hand and stepped back, his expression suddenly solemn. "What about you? I suppose the only reason you like me is because I'm a dashing bandit."

"You're not *that* dashing," she informed him. "Especially when you're under some dark-minion spell and staring all googly-eyed—"

"Leaving the past aside," Bain interrupted, "I want to ask you a question."

"Go ahead."

Bain took a deep breath before he spoke. "May I court you, Your Most Unique and Royal Highness?"

Meg was starting to enjoy this. "Oh, probably. If the prime minister doesn't throw you in the dungeon first."

He smiled. "Fair enough."

And with that understanding, they went off to find the others.

From the top of a tower somewhere deep in the enchanted forest, a song floated like green scum on the surface of a pond. Actually, the song sounded like a cross between an irate weasel and a laryngitic mermaid who'd eaten some bad fish, with maybe a handful of rusty knives and forks being scraped along a gravestone tossed in for good measure. Most people wouldn't have called it a song.

A prince riding through the forest on a great white charger heard the singing and made a face. "What is *that*?" he asked no one in particular. Being a brave as well as a curious young man, he rode in the direction of the noise to find out.

He followed the song until he came to a clearing, where he discovered a tall tower. The music stopped abruptly. "Hello?" the prince called. There was no answer. The prince rode in a circle around the tower, but it had no windows or doors.

"Is anyone up there?" the prince yelled, but no one replied. "Hello?" the prince said again.

A hollow voice filled the clearing. "Seeeek the magic swooorrd."

"There's a magic sword?" the prince asked. "Where?"

"In the heeaaart of the fooorrressst liessss the swooorrd."

"Magic sword. Heart of the forest. Got it," the prince said with a decisive nod. He spun his mount around, then spun it right back again, causing the steed to give a whinny of protest. "Wait. Is there a damsel involved?"

"Of coouurrssse."

"Good. Thanks for the tip." The prince urged his white stallion out of the clearing, back into the forest. The sound of hoofbeats soon faded away.

A contented sigh could be heard from the top of the tower. A face appeared at the window—a wrinkled old man's face with a long gray beard (though not nearly as long as Spinach's braid). Quorlock smiled. "Now, that's more like it," he said, leaning on the windowsill and looking out over the enchanted forest, a place filled with unidentifiable green-eyed creatures, a magic sword, various squirrels of questionable origin, the too-quiet body of a dead witch, a demon pit, a couple of changeable streams, a damsel in distress, a white stag, and a myriad of other mysteries.

EPILOGUE

THE QUESTERS TOOK THE LONG WAY HOME, skirting around the enchanted forest, which meant they had only two or three more adventures along the way instead of five or six. Even so, Meg ran into a helpful fish, a friendly bird, and a rather uppity fox, all of whom repaid their debts of honor with varying degrees of success and enthusiasm.

In time Meg's bedraggled party arrived back at the castle in Greeve, where Meg had a joyous reunion with her parents and gave her mother an attack of nerves by telling her about the sorceress and the giant in great detail. Then when Meg introduced Bain—well! Despite Meg's best efforts at diplomacy, Queen Istilda wandered about the court with her beautiful face pale and drawn for some time before she rallied and began telling everyone that Bain was really a prince in disguise. Needless to say, Bain was *not* thrown in the dungeon, although unruffleable Guard Captain Hanak looked ruffled for at least twenty minutes when he heard the news, and the prime minister pouted for days afterward.

Lex settled back into his ever-changing house, which was made of blue glass when he arrived, to read his new books, a large mug of hot chocolate near at hand. Spinach moved into the tower where Meg had once been sequestered because it was where she felt most comfortable. Her hair grew to the exact length needed to reach from the tower window to the ground. However, Cam used the stairs when he came to bring her bouquets of vegetables and answer her many questions. Ever observant, Dilly noticed what Cam was up to within half a day. Whereupon she made a smug little face and said, "See?" to Meg.

Of course, Dilly and Nort sometimes went to the market together, bickering every step of the way, which caused Meg to make the same sort of face as Dilly's, though she kept herself from saying "See?" out loud.

Dilly had gone far beyond saying "See?" when she had met Meg and Bain walking back along the edge of the enchanted forest with a look of mutual surprise about them. Her expressions of delight and horror were still ringing in Meg's ears, as were Queen Istilda's initial histrionics, King Stromgard's gloomy speeches, and the courtiers' gossip.

Meg listened to everyone, then went off to visit

Gorba. She discovered that the witch had learned to get along with her new kitten by the simple act of catering to Miss Mystery's every whim. To Meg's relief, Gorba was still an incurable romantic: she thought the idea of a semi-reformed bandit courting Meg was simply splendid.

Not long after the travelers returned, Meg found a quiet moment to give Spinach the picture in the pink frame and tell her what she and Lex had seen in the forest that night. "I thought so," was all Spinach said, though her face said a lot more.

Good old Crobbs melted back into Hanak's troop of guards. Everyone soon learned that it was best not to talk to him about squirrels. The guardsmen held a memorial service for their lost companions, which Meg and her friends attended, sitting in the back.

There was some talk about Lex coming up with a squirrel-rescuing spell, but so far, he was still experimenting on mice.

When Meg introduced Bain to Master Zolis, the swordmaster offered to teach him swordplay. Bain responded to this signal honor by saying, "I don't need any lessons," to which Master Zolis replied that he would be happy to show the young man otherwise. Much to Meg's amusement, Bain and the swordmaster were pretty evenly matched. In fact, both men seemed pleased to have encountered somebody worth sparring with. Bain ended up teaching several of the students on Master Zolis's long list of eager pupils.

Bain also taught Meg how to dance without stepping on his toes, a task Master Deedle had despaired of. Meg retaliated by teaching Bain every single one of Mistress Mintz's eleven curtsies. When that lady found out, she fell into a state of permanent dismay, having never managed to acquire such an impolite thing as a sense of humor.

Weeks passed, and Meg wondered how her runaway dragon was getting along. Was he truly well hidden, out there in the mountains beyond the enchanted forest? Was he getting enough goats to eat? Was he burning any villages, or taking up any other bad habits?

Then one afternoon Meg heard people screaming and running. She ran to the window and caught a glimpse of sunlight flashing on red-and-gold scales as Laddy buzzed the castle. *Thbbbbbhbt!* Meg heard in her head.

Meet me on the roof! Meg called to her dragon.

Next she hurried to tell Hanak about her guest before her father could get into a dudgeon. The level-headed guard captain agreed to explain things to the archers and calm the courtiers. That settled, Meg stopped by her chambers to retrieve a very important sheet of parchment before she ran up four flights of stairs to perch on the castle roof beside Laddy.

Did you miss me? he asked.

Of course! Tell me everything.

So Laddy told her about flying with eagles, experimenting with dragon magic—*I can make myself invisible now!*—exploring hidden canyons, and spying on the kingdoms on the other side of the mountains.

I hope you're eating right, Meg said.

Mountain goats are good, and so are deer.

Any sausages?

Laddy smiled a long toothy smile. *Once. But I left a gold coin to pay for them.*

Good boy.

Have you thought about it any more? he asked.

Your name? Yes. Meg was prepared this time. She pulled the list out of her pocket and began to read. *Sorgalorn?*

No.

Hainlesek?

No.

Trelenariane? It was hard to say that one.

No.

Fantastanoff?

That's ridiculous, Laddy said.

All right. How about Drackslither?

Too snaky.

Aurumgelve? Meg suggested.

No.

Crimsontail?

Mmm—no.

Teethslicer?

That sounds like slicing up teeth, Laddy said, trying not to seem disdainful.

Merenol?

A wizard's name. You're not very good at this, are you?

I'm trying, she told him. *What about you?*

I have one idea.

Why didn't you say so?

I wanted to hear yours first. Laddy laughed in her mind.

Fine. Go on, then.

Fireshine, he said cautiously.

Oh!

What do you mean, "Oh"? Laddy sounded worried.

I mean "Oh, that's perfect"! Meg told him. *You look like fire when you fly.*

I can make fire, too.

It really was perfect. So Meg and her dragon, who wasn't exactly her dragon anymore, sat on top of the castle and talked until the sun began to go down. Laddy showed her how he could become invisible, and Meg told him all of the castle gossip. She had the cook send up three trays of sausages for a snack partway through.

When the day was almost gone, Laddy—Fireshine— lifted off the roof, a dragon made of flame in the last light of the setting sun. The fire faded into darkness as he flew away south to make sure his gold was still waiting for him in his mountain lair.

Quests don't always turn out like you think they will, Meg thought as she ran down the stairs to see if Master Zolis had taught Bain a lesson today, or the other way round. Even so, she decided, going on a quest and coming home again was just as good as she had always thought it would be.

AUTHOR'S NOTE ABOUT FAIRY TALES

Most of you have probably seen *Enchanted*, *Shrek*, *Ella Enchanted*, and a bunch of Disney movies based on fairy tales. You've probably read a dozen or so well-known stories such as "Little Red Riding Hood" and "Sleeping Beauty," too—but what about "Iron Hans," "The Golden Bird," or "Mother Hulda"? I discovered the seemingly secret world of fairy tales when I was about eight: I could go to the library and check out collections of stories from all over the world! Sometimes my family even gave me fairy tale collections for my birthday. I still own the book of tales from the Arabian Nights my grandma gave me years ago. That's where I met Aladdin, Sinbad, and clever Morgiana, although my favorite story was actually about a magic bird and some cucumbers stuffed with pearls.

Those German story collectors, the Brothers Grimm, introduced me to wonderful European tales. I particularly liked a comical horror story about a youth who could not shudder, so he set out to learn the meaning of fear. In a book of stories from Japan, I learned that Japanese fairy tales don't always have happy endings and that Tom Thumb has a counterpart called Issun-bōshi (Little One-Inch), a tiny yet fierce boy who wants to be a samurai warrior. I also read books of myths and legends, especially stories about colorful tricksters such as the Native American Coyote and the West African spider, Anansi. When I read a collection of Russian tales, I discovered that the scariest witch ever is Baba Yaga, who lives in a house that has chicken feet, surrounded by a fence made of human bones.

I guess it shouldn't be too surprising that I grew up to write books like *The Runaway Dragon*, in which I have fun playing with typical European fairy tales. Let me give you a quick look at some of the stories I had in mind as I wrote it. For example, maybe you're wondering why the girl in the tower is named Spinach. Of course, Spinach's story is based on "Rapunzel," and that fairy tale begins with a pregnant woman who is craving a leaf vegetable from a witch's garden. The common name for the vegetable is corn salad, but one of its other names is *rapunzel*. The witch catches the woman's husband stealing from her and demands his baby as payment. Naturally, the baby is named after the fate-altering vegetable! The witch then puts the child in a doorless tower in the middle of the woods, where she visits her by climbing up her long hair. Rapunzel finally escapes from the tower after a handsome prince hears her singing, though she has further troubles with the angry witch before she gets a happy ending.

Like *The Runaway Dragon*, a lot of fairy tales involve quests. In European stories, the hero is usually a youngest son whose two older brothers are selfish and proud. First each of the older brothers sets out to seek his fortune. When the brothers meet an old beggar on the road, they refuse to give him (or her) any food—and end up lost or enchanted. In contrast, the kindhearted youngest son willingly shares his bread with the beggar, who turns out to have magical powers or useful information for our hero. In the Grimms' story "The Golden Goose," a little gray man accepts bread from youngest son Simpleton, then advises him to cut down a certain tree in the forest. There Simpleton finds a golden goose that will make a princess laugh. The little gray man and others like him inspired my character Quorlock, who takes his role as a magical adviser far too seriously.

Quorlock coaches Meg on being kind to animals because in many tales a hero who treats animals with compassion later benefits from their help. "The White Snake," another story from the Brothers Grimm, tells of a young man who learns the language of animals and sets off to see the world. Along the way, he finds three fishes out of the water and puts them back in the pond, turns aside on the path so as not to destroy an ants' nest, and kills his horse to feed three young ravens who are starving. (Poor horse!) Later, when the youth tries to win the hand of a princess, he is given three impossible tasks: fetch a gold ring from the bottom of the sea, sort out ten sacks of millet seed that have been thrown in the grass, and bring back a golden apple from the tree of life. The fishes, the ants, and the ravens come and help the youth complete his tasks.

Animal helpers also show up in a Norwegian story called "The Giant Who Had No Heart in His Body," as does another intriguing plot point that comes up briefly in my book (when Meg and the servant women are storming the fortress). Boots, the youngest of seven princes, helps a raven, a salmon, and a wolf during his journey. Then he rides the wolf to a giant's house where a princess is held captive. The giant is invincible for the simple reason that he does not keep his heart inside his body. Boots hides while the princess pesters the giant to find out his secret. Finally she learns that the heart is kept in an egg inside a duck that swims in a well inside a church on a distant island in the middle of a lake. With the help of his three animal friends, Boots is able to retrieve the heart. Then he squeezes it, killing the giant. He not only rescues the princess, but also his six older brothers and their six princess fiancées, who have been turned to stone by the giant. Notice that this giant, like Lorgley Comprost, knows some magic!

The people in another fairy tale turn into animals

when they drink from a stream, though much grander animals than squirrels. In the Grimms' version, "Brother and Sister," two children run away from their wicked stepmother into the forest, but she is a witch and has cast spells on all of the streams. The first stream warns them that it will turn whoever drinks it into a tiger. The brother wants to drink, but his sister begs him not to, afraid he will turn into a tiger and devour her. The next stream they find says it will turn anyone who drinks it into a wolf, and again the boy resists his thirst. By the third stream, though, the boy is so thirsty that he drinks the water, turning into a deer. His sister finds a little hut in the wood and lives there, caring for her brother the deer. But when a king comes hunting, the deer longs for the thrill of being chased. The king and his men hunt the young stag for three days, eventually tracking the enchanted creature to the hut where the girl lives. The king falls in love with the girl and, after further complications, the deer's enchantment is ended.

Speaking of deer, there's a reason Harry Potter's patronus (and his father's animagus form) is a white stag. And if you've read C. S. Lewis's *The Lion, the Witch, and the Wardrobe*, you may recall that the hunt for the white stag is what leads the four Pevensie children back from Narnia to our world in the final pages of the book. Ms. Rowling and Mr. Lewis were no doubt inspired by the British legend in which King Arthur's knights pursue a magical white stag. The hunt for an otherworldly deer turns up in legends from other countries, too. For example, in Celtic legends, the white stag was supposed to be able to lead hunters into Fairyland. The pursuit of a magical deer is part of the legend of the founding of Hungary, and the white stag is also associated with tales of the elusive unicorn. In most of these stories and legends, men are the only ones who pursue the stag, though that's probably because in the time the tales are set, the rulers and hunters were usually men. Rarely does anyone actually *catch* the white stag, but the hunt for it represents the search for wisdom. The appearance of the magical stag is also thought to signal the beginning of a quest or adventure—like Meg's!

ACKNOWLEDGMENTS

A special thanks to my writing friends Marsha Skrypuch, Karen Dyer, and Linda Gerber for their feedback and encouragement on this book and many other projects. I'd also like to thank my editor, Janine O'Malley, and her compatriot Lisa Graff for their very helpful input.